# Catherine T.L. Hodges

# Jordan's River

# Jordan's River

## Catherine T L Hodges

Wider Perspectives Publishing, 2020 Hampton Roads, Va.

# DEDICATIONS

First, I have to say that this book has been in the works for over fifteen years, so I have to thank God for blessing me with the gift of craft through writing. On the very same level, I have to pay much respect to the late Mrs. Maya Angelou for her touch, her words, and her encouragement when I was just a young child before I even knew I had the heart to write.

I could dedicate this to everyone who played any kind of role in getting this project off the ground, but that would be another entire book, so I'll limit that list. Mom, I know you are reading this from heaven, and I know you would be so proud of me for sticking with this until the end...regardless of the many obstacles, so I dedicate this to your memory.

Precious, you have been here since I typed the very first stroke and have become kin to the characters within. You've challenged my motives, questioned my plot, and laughed at the oddest times forcing me to revisit many scenarios for the better. You have cooked and served me meals at my computer so I could continue to work on this. I definitely dedicate Jordan's River to you for your diligence, hard work, and loyalty throughout this entire project.

Keith, when I wrote the first draft of Jordan's River, it was in 2004; we did not meet until 2020. You walked right into my life as my Jordan, and in the finalization process, you've kept me positive and pushed me forward to get it done. This is also dedicated to you, my love!

# PROLOGUE

You would think that the first week of being homeless on the streets of Hampton Roads in Virginia would have been the hardest, but, just as with everything else in my twisted and sorted life, this would prove to be another backwards venture for me. My last two weeks were probably the worst two weeks of my life, and I had nothing to fall back on but a hope and a prayer. Granted, I was homeless partially because I chose to be. I was a grown woman with children of my own and had a list of rules set for a teenager to follow, and following the rules of the house were not leaving a pleasant taste in my mouth. I really had nowhere to go. I mean, I had friends and distant family, but I didn't want to impose on them, you know? Some of my upbringing was so strong in me that I couldn't break away from it, so I chose to sleep in my outdated, in-desperate-need-of-repair Ford LTD Crown Victoria, and wherever I parked it for that night was my address of choice.

Two years of deciding whether I was sleeping on the front seat or the back seat was beyond taking its toll, and working the drive-thru at Burger King didn't afford me too many other options. Hell, I couldn't afford to pay rent at a free orphanage with what I was making. My three children were living with my mother in Cavalier Manor in Portsmouth, and I made sure I got by there to see them at least once a day.

I prided myself on being a good mother. I was there for the backyard barbecues, last minute checks before going to school, and the late nights playing Monopoly. I even spent the night a couple of times, and we called it a family sleep-over. My children were always happy to see me, but I think I was more thrilled to see them, and every day was like seeing them for the first time in years. These babies of mine were, and still are, the greatest.

I knew that I had to make some changes, so I applied for a housekeeping job at the local hospital, where the service was so bad, it was affectionately known as Murderville, USA, but the pay was excellent for what I needed, and the staff was too kind to me and my situation. Working in housekeeping overnight on the fifth floor, there were always a great deal of empty rooms. So, the charge nurse would let me stay in a room as long as I cleaned it and was out before 7:00 the next morning. I usually tried to be out by 6:00. I didn't want to press my luck. It was like free room and board, and afforded me the opportunity to save some real money for a nice place for myself and the children!

We were told that it should take ten minutes to clean an empty room, twenty minutes to clean a patient's room and thirty to minutes to clean a discharge. I think I had a total of four discharges the entire time I was employed there. As far as cleaning the rooms, working overnight, we only went in rooms on request as to not disturb the sleeping patients. After all, they were in the hospital to heal. Constantly going in and out of their room, especially with chemicals, was intrusive. I would turn a twenty minute cleaning project into a seven minute wonder. The secret was to take everything you needed into the room, avoiding the in and out; just by doing that, you cut out eight minutes. Then, develop a system that works for you. Mine was simple: start at the furthest point (the bathroom) and work your way back to the exit door.

After three months at the hospital, I was ready to start looking at apartments. I needed to be with my babies, and they needed to be with me. I found a downstairs unit in Abbey's Place located downtown. With my limp, I didn't need to be fighting stairs every day. Now, it wasn't the best looking apartment complex in town, but it was clean, well-kept, and provided shelter for my family. They were affordable, and made to make our own rules that weren't quite so unreasonable. Although it wasn't the safest neighborhood, it quickly became home, and my little ones acclimated to their surroundings. The transition from the grassy play yard at my mother's house was replaced with an asphalt covered parking lot for the kids. But it was home, and that's what mattered most.

Personally, I never have been what you may call, that I-N-D-E-P-E-N-D-E-N-T type woman; although I have never relied on a man to pay my bills, feed me and/or children, or do anything else for me for that matter, especially bust a nutt. Between my toys and my fingers, I had some amazing tricks that achieved maximum satisfaction yet to be matched by any man. I needed a man around for the companionship, for the spooning, for the little light kisses on the back of the neck when I'm washing dishes, for the cat calls when I'm scrubbing the floor, for the hot and steamy sex in the hot and steamy shower. Hell, yeah, I demanded that he work and pull his weight in my house. I demanded that he be an upstanding kind of guy that my son could mimic and my daughters could look up to. Call it being hard, but I don't accept or take care of free-loaders, and I always have the best interest of my children at heart. I grew to be hard from my experiences on the streets. You had to fight daily for what you wanted and even what you already had. My little family wasn't rich by a long shot. As a matter of fact, we struggled, but I wasn't about to let some outsider come in and take advantage of the little that we *did* have.

I think it was a Monday afternoon that I stopped at the convenience gas station to fill up my little, white Chrysler LeBaron for the week. Yeah, I upgraded! I saw that the lottery jackpot was pretty high and figured, "even if I don't get the big jackpot, a few thousand right now would be the type of miracle that I need." So I sashayed inside and paid for two jackpot tickets. $2.00. I stood there at the counter and placed the tickets in my rarely used wallet, and as I opened the wallet, I saw a $20.00 bill that I had tucked away for hard times. These were hard times, so I bought two more tickets. The drawing wasn't until the next evening, so I tossed the second set of tickets in a hidden compartment in the car. You know, one of those little spots that no one would think to look in if they broke in. Hell, I would even forget to look there when I needed that in-the-couch cash.

I scurried home to be with my babies and hear all about their day away from me. It was what I looked forward to after being switched to day shift on my job. I mean, I earned it. I pulled doubles, covered other people's shifts, and helped pass all sorts of inspections with my 'exemplary' cleaning. That 'exemplary' cleaning got me Employee of the Year four times in a row. Lack of cleanliness was not the reason for the name "Murderville"!

I wish I could tell you that I was an instant multi-millionaire overnight, but neither of my two tickets was a match. I wasn't devastated, but I was a little let down. Five months went by and no one claimed the $472 million dollar jackpot... from any of the participating states. Later that same day, the Virginia lottery released a press statement notifying the public that the void time was drawing near for the unclaimed ticket and *that one winning* ticket was purchased at the same store where I got my tickets. Then it all came back to me. I purchased four tickets, not two! The trick now was to remember what I had done with the other two tickets...

*7 – 14 – 32 – 41 – 43 Jackpot Play Ball 2*

I stood in the office of the Official Virginia Lottery Commission, and I was stunned motionless. I couldn't move. I just kept repeating the numbers that had no real significance to me. I just randomly filled in boxes. There was no method, no plotting, no birthdays, no special dates, no nothing tying these numbers to anything in my life other than the fact that these arbitrary numbers would change my life forever.

It came out just like that! They showed the number on the board just like that! I showed up in Hampton with the winning ticket two days before it expired, and my whole everything changed...

# *1*

I woke up to the smell of bacon, eggs with cheese, and toast filling the air. There was a distinct aroma of citrus as well, but I couldn't tell if it was orange or tangerine. My youngest daughter was quite the master in the kitchen, and I did everything I knew to encourage her to continue on her culinary path. I knew this was her calling. Jenique was very familiar with every aspect of the kitchen and could whip a hearty meal together with very few ingredients in no time. I waited until she was seven until I introduced her to the kitchen, and she fell in place. She said she wanted to own and operate her very own restaurant wanted it to be "good food at a price that poor parents could afford to feed their children". Trust me; this little lady was wise beyond her years because she remembered the struggles we went through.

After getting my personal morning started (which consisted of a couple of rounds of masturbation and showering), I joined Jenique for breakfast and we exchanged our daily to-do lists. As usual, I had nothing special planned but spending a few hours at my homeless facility and the rest of the day at my little crochet boutique in the dilapidating Tower Mall.

The mall had been in existence since 1973, and was on its way out after 25 years of Montgomery Wards, J. M. Fields, Chuck E. Cheese, Chick-Fil-A, PayLess, the A B C store, the ever-packed movie theater, and all the other hangout spots. After about the mid-nineties, the mall became a hanging ground for preteens and wanna-be gang members. It was more like a breeding ground for trouble after all the stores closed down for the night. But my little boutique was very close to the main entrance and the security office, so I faired pretty well.

Forgive my rudeness. I guess I should tell you that my name is Crystal Lackner. I am the founder, co-designer, and owner of The Lackner Centers, facilities designed to house the homeless and underprivileged, offering them employment and teaching them life skills before reintroducing them back into mainstream society, with a mission of succeeding in life.

It's been four years since I built my first center here in Portsmouth where the old Craddock High School once stood. I can usually make it to the building in as little as four minutes driving with no traffic and not getting caught by any lights. But there are those gorgeous fall and spring mornings that call for that long meditative walk in to the facility. I bolt from my home on Crystal Lake Drive down Rotunda Avenue and onto Greenwood Drive. From there, turning right onto Maupin Avenue, then left onto Fairview Circle North. Once crossing Deep Creek Boulevard onto Bellhaven Road, it's pretty much a wrap from there. I knew that I would be spending a great deal of time here, so I had my office set up like an apartment complete with bedroom, bath, and even an eat-in kitchen. This came in handy on those days that I really didn't want to go out for lunch or had an impromptu meeting in the office and needed something quick and easy or elegant for the smaller meetings. Jenique was not the only one who could burn in the kitchen. She got her skills honest because my grandmother passed them down to me as well.

Although my facility was extremely lucrative, it was run by a government funded program. So, I run a tight ship. I give all my residents the tools they need to succeed and try to keep them motivated with a positive outlook toward their future. I involve them in training courses for long-term success instead of shipping them out and offering a revolving door. Don't get me wrong, but if they need to come back, provided we have the room, they are more than welcome to re-enter the program without scrutiny.

Since the groundbreaking of the first building in 1999, there have been six other Lackner Centers erected, one in each of the seven cities. Each facility holds a maximum of 248 individuals in apartment-type settings except the latest one built in Suffolk. That building holds 325 individuals because it is the largest city in the state (in mass) and the homeless rate is higher there as well.

Let me back up just a little. I did hit the lottery for $472 million dollars, and once they ate up their portion in taxes and fees, I waltzed away with $350 million. Too much to squander away in one of my lifetimes. My first order of business was to pay off all my outstanding debt, medical bills and student loans, and even though I wanted to be as nasty with my creditors as they had been with me over the years and pay them all in unwrapped pennies, the good in me wouldn't allow me do that. So, I stroked each one of them a check and attached two business cards in case they happened across someone who needed what my facility has to offer. I believe the saying is 'kill 'em with kindness', and that's exactly what I did.

      After tying up a few more odds and ends like rebuilding my mother's home, setting up funds for my children, and buying my home that I designed and had built from the drawing of the blueprints to the tacking on the roof cap in Crystal Lake, I opened a little crochet boutique, Kitteez Kreationz; specializing in personalized crochet. I have to admit this is where I spent most of my time watching television, talking to clients, and crocheting. I was just a phone call away from home and the facility if needed. It worked! Jenique and my oldest daughter, Laticia, spent time in the shoppe when Laticia wasn't getting her college on. Marco, my son, worked in the little convenience mart located inside the Portsmouth facility. He was my back-up whenever I was away and they needed something quickly. He knew the ins and outs and, if any problems surfaced, he knew how to handle them.

      I still tried to make sure we did as many things together as possible. We went fishing at least twice a month during the warm months, we went to amusement parks in and out of the state, and we frequented one of the four time shares down on the Outer Banks bi-weekly from spring through autumn. Even though I hit the lottery - big, I always tried to express the importance of making one's own way in life to my children. I never wanted them to depend on anyone or any system. The money I put aside for them was not available to them until their 21$^{st}$ birthdays. They were getting a weekly allowance, which was less than the interest accrued on their accounts, so they were still earning money on top of their money. They also had to work to afford living and had to pay for their rooming and other amenities. Although I would redeposit the funds that they paid me on a monthly basis into their individual accounts, they were learning the importance of paying bills and paying them on time. There were a stiff penalties for late payments, and I would make them feel it – deeply! I never wanted them to experience homelessness, destitution, or having to 'rob Peter to pay Paul'! I wanted them to know good, sound decision-making. I wanted them to understand every decision you make in life comes with a consequence, whether good or bad. I also wanted them to understand that this was just money, not life, and it came with great responsibility, not pride and conceit. If they squandered it away, they were just ass out.

Jordan's River

6

# 2

After leaving the shop later than usual that evening, I wanted to stop by Giant Open Air Market and pick up a nice salad, but I let time slip away from me, and the salad bar was closed for the evening. Sounded like fresh produce to me, so I piddled around in the veggie area gathering everything I thought I needed to make my own version of the fresh garden salad I so desired. There was the lettuce, cheese, onions, cukes, tomatoes, spinach, carrots, red cabbage - the whole shebang. I even had the almonds and the sunflower kernels.

Noticing there was a special on the regular, green cabbage, and Laticia absolutely loves the stuff, I thought I'd grab a couple of heads for tomorrow night's dinner since she was home from school for a spell. And, there he was! This guy! He was milk chocolate and chiseled; plain and pleasing; flawless and fabulous. He caught my attention right away. This man was standing there at the cabbage lightly squeezing them, examining each head for any flaws. I felt like he was looking for himself in the cabbage. Hell, I wished he was looking for me the way he was caressing each one so gently yet with such a firm hold! He must've had ten heads in his basket already. All I could think was that he had a huge family and loved cabbage, or he had an issue, maybe an obsession. Either way, I found myself mocking him in looking for the perfect cabbage.

I don't even know this cat, but I felt like he definitely knew something that I didn't know. Hell, he's rubbing off on me already.

He broke the silence with "Have you tried that steamed with fresh onions a hint of garlic?"

"No. I was actually picking out a couple to go with tomorrow night's dinner."

"No, I was referring to the red one! Have you tried it steamed with fresh on..."

"No, I haven't! I mean, I have only used the red ones for salads and coleslaw. Don't get me wrong, I know you can cook them. I just never did it."

"You never did it!?" Then he erupted into hearty laughter.

I didn't find it too amusing until I replayed the conversation in my head. Call me slow. How stupid I must have sounded. I think the redness of my face showed I was truly embarrassed by the inability to catch the joke instantly. He apologized, explaining he had had a very stressful day and needed the light humor. He did assured me that he wasn't making fun of me, but it sure felt like he was at that moment.

I found myself standing there in conversation with this man for the better part of an hour, and I didn't even know his name, so I slid in an informal introduction in, "Chris, and you are...?"

"My name is Jordan, Jordan Hines. It's a pleasure to meet you, Chris. You know, I could give you some salad ideas to share with your husband and children, if you'd like!"

How cute! He was fishing to see if I was married. I didn't know whether to play the game or to save him the trouble. "No, no, no! I'm not married, not even in a committed relationship. Hell, I'm so single it's me that's stamped on the penny!" Okay, maybe I gave a little bit too much away. Hell, I must've sounded so desperate.

It felt good that both of us were laughing this time. I made a funny, and someone else laughed!

"Well, Chris, I can make that salad for you one evening when you're available, if you'd like."

Now he's flirting for real? "I'd like...very much, sir!"

We exchanged numbers and set the time for our date. I don't know if I was more excited about the fact I had a date or the fact I had a date I wasn't paying for.

The six-minute drive home was an interesting one. I think I sat in the driveway for about ten minutes absorbing the details of my encounter in the produce section. He was charming. He was different. He was so fine. I realized I had soaked the seat of my tan, linen pants just thinking about being folded in his leaves while taking in his stalk slowly, allowing him to excrete through the core of his vein. Yes, Mr. Jordan Hines, you can come and serve me any time.

I finally went in the house undiscovered, so I was safe. I quickly scurried into my room because I could hear Jenique up and about, and the last thing I needed was for her to see that huge soaked area of my pants. She's the inquisitive type, and she would have been asking far too many questions. I closed my room door, turned on my Luther Vandross, and pretended to be a private dancer for Mr. Hines. I mean, a girl can dream, right? I was grinding and twisting, shaking and twerking, and the damn phone rang.

Of course I wondered who it was. Only the Center would call me this time of the evening, and that usually meant there was a problem, but the caller ID read *CALLER UNKNOWN*. I answered in my fake British accent only to find out that it was Jordan, himself. Turning into an instant teenager, I giggled for thirty seconds before composing myself enough to have a decent conversation with him.

I really did not expect him to call so quickly. I must have made one hell of an impression. He wasted no time reaching out!

Jordan and I spent a great deal of time on the phone as people do in the newness of relationships, even the ones that fail. I like to call it 'The Learning Phase'. This is the time you spend learning everything you can about each other so there are no future surprises or disappointments. He was fascinating, interesting, and interested in me. I think I was most amazed at the fact that he talked, but he listened as well. It was like he was using an egg timer or something because we got equal input time, which was awesome. It was definitely something I was not accustomed to since I am such a talker.

His voice was soothing. I mean, he had that perfect play-with-my-pussy voice thing going on. It wasn't raspy; it was just a sultry, sexy, confident baritone. It made me want to tear his bone up. WHEW! I guess it was the dog in me! Ha-ha

I was really trying to be a good girl with Jordan, but after four years of being celibate, I was so ready to make lo...Fuck that! I was past ready to fuck like the zombie apocalypse had come and gone and Jordan and I are the only two people left to repopulate the world.

# *3*

Three days after meeting Jordan, I invited him to my home so that he could prepare that salad he offered to make for me. When he showed up twenty minutes early, I was very impressed, not only with his impeccable timing, but he looked amazing. He was wearing a pair of Khakis and a nice sky-blue Polo shirt that complimented his muscular build. His glasses made him look very astute and sexy along with that fresh shave and trim, and his head had sheen ... bald definitely suited him. He was slightly bow-legged, and that is such a turn-on for me. My heart skipped a few beats, my nipples stood at attention, and my silks were instantly moistened. WOW! I felt like I had hit the lottery all over again.

I had already set the table for two, and he made himself at home in my large, eat-in kitchen. The Chardonnay was chilling in the freezer, and the cheesecake was setting in the refrigerator. Alicia Keys' "Falling" was playing in the background, and I had started to sing a few bars out loud displaying my vocal talents. He was totally enthralled and captivated. I guess my years in the church choir paid off. At one point, Jordan stopped all of his preparations and just listened. That attention made me feel sort of accomplished and majorly special.

I wanted to help him, so I volunteered to cut up some of the ingredients for him, but he was sternly adamant about doing it all himself...he said it was his treat to me. I loved watching him maneuver around my kitchen like he belonged there, but not as much as I loved the delicious salad. YUM! The wine went perfectly with it, and the cheesecake was to die for. Dinner was truly succulent and divine, and the presence of his company made it that much mo' better.

"So, what do you do, Chris?"

Not wanting to scare him off or have him tagging along for the wrong reason, I gave him as little information as possible. I wanted to be sure that he was into me and not my fortune, but I didn't want to come across as a needy skeeze either. Those had been two reasons I had not dated in so long. It's not that I didn't try, but I quickly learned that the few I had attempted to date were in it for what they could get out of it... financially!

"I work at The Lackner Center and a little shoppe called Kitteez Kreationz located in the mall," I finally responded.

"I've heard of the shoppe. As a matter of fact, I've seen it! It's right there by that little pretzel shop, right? They specialize in personalized crochet, right? I was interested in getting a couple of afghans made for my girls. How do I go about getting that done?" His face was so sincere, and he had the cutest dimple on his right cheek. Hell, he even knew my mission statement.

He sported a quarter karat diamond stud in his right earlobe, and he had a tattoo of two roses on his left forearm with the words Duchess and Princess in them. I was fascinated by tattoos, and I knew that most of them came with a very special and endearing meaning. I wondered what "Duchess and Princess" meant to him.

"Well, you have to talk to the owner about any personalized orders; she handles all of that."

"I want Duchess and Princess on the afghans along with their birthdate ... December 2."

"REALLY!? That's my birthday, too!" I volunteered enthusiastically.

"I have twin daughters. Their names are Duchess and Princess." He chuckled for a bit. "I guess I have high expectations for them, huh?"

He bragged about his girls for about twenty minutes or so, complimenting their strengths and outspokenness. He said that he loved that about them, and he knew that no one would ever be able to take advantage of them as long as they were true to who they were.

He also spoke highly of their mother and how helpful she was in making sure that the girls were able to adjust to having an active father in their life and a loving step-father. It was a separated home, but a united family where all parties did much more than just get along.

I tried to learn as much as I could without interrupting with questions until I realized that I knew nothing of why he was so familiar with foods ... or why he had so many heads of cabbage in his basket the night we met at the grocery store. "So, Jordan, I noticed the night we met that you had a lot of cabbage in your basket. What do you do for a living?"

"I'm the Executive Chef at Lock's Point in the Great Bridge section of Chesapeake. It's located right off of Bat..."

"Battlefield Boulevard...I'm familiar! I love their smoked salmon and blackened beans. As a matter of fact, I'm in that restaurant at least twice a week. There is one thing that I don't like ... that small glass they serve tea in. It's a waste! It looks more like a test tube, but I guess that's one way to ensure the server makes frequent trips around to the table."

Again, we shared laughter.

We both got up to gather and wash the dishes, and, again, Jordan insisted that this night was a total treat for me and that I should just sit back and relax while he did all the work. Hey, who wouldn't soak that up?

I tried not to stare, but he was looking too delicious not to. He asked no questions and went right to work, and I think I started feeling a tad bit guilty and asked if I could at least dry the dishes and put them away, but since I love an open concept, the placement of the cleaned dishes was easy.

After he finished the dishes, he poured another couple of glasses of wine and we watched, mocked, and critiqued *"The Color Purple"*. He was the perfect gentleman, and I felt so comfortable in his arms while sitting on the couch. At one point, I remember thinking that this man must've seen this movie just as many times as I have because he knew just about all the lines. A few times, we would even get up and act out a scene or two. Our date was perfect.

When the evening drew to an end, he left, and all I could do was thank his parents for raising him to be the man he was, thank God for creating him to be as fine as he was, and I was secretly thanking Jordan for being as interested in me as he seemed to be. He left with the same confident walk as when he came. Those bowed legs, though!

As I climbed into my king-sized bed waiting for my nightly call, I chuckled at the memories that were just made. It had been a long time since a man was responsible for putting a smile on my face before I slumbered. Then my thoughts were pleasantly interrupted by the phone ringing...

"Hello!"

"Hey, I just wanted to let you know that I made it in okay, and ... I miss you already. I know that sounds a bit cheesy, but you're beautiful...inside and out, and I hope this was the first of many evenings together."

Biting my bottom lip, I concurred. "I enjoyed your company as well, Jordan. You are quite the gentleman, and I appreciate you for that."

"Chris, don't you think for one moment that it was easy keeping my hands off of you. I mean, you're a beautiful and sexy woman, indeed! You were the perfect hostess, and you sing like an angel, but when we were sitting on the couch together..."

We both chuckled and trailed off into conversation still getting to know each other and comparing histories before we teetered off merrily into la-la land...I in my Crystal Lake home and Jordan in his Camelot home. We were so close, but we were far enough away that maintaining was easy.

# Jordan's River

# *4*

The next evening, Jordan showed up at the shoppe and asked if I had talked to the owner about the special request on his behalf. I assured him the owner knew about it, but needed more details. Information like colors, sizes, and the expected pick-up date was needed to complete the ordering process. I took the information to the back office as if I were taking them to someone else, did my own calculations, and came back with the estimate and deposit amount.

His eyes lit up like Christmas trees, and he was way too giddy. You would have thought that he had just received the deal of a lifetime. "Can I leave the deposit right now? I mean, there really isn't a rush. I'm just so excited: I know they'll love them, and they'll be completed in plenty of time for their birthday. So, she's cool with starting right away?"

"I'm sure she'll probably wait until tomorrow to start, but I'm sure she'll get right on it! I don't think she has anyone ahead of you right now."

"Oh, I could kiss her right now - and you!"

Out of the blue, his arms were nestled on my hips, and his lips were pressed ever so gently against mine. All I could do was close my eyes and go with it. His lips felt like pure cotton. I wanted to feel that fineness all over my body. When our lips finally unlocked, we just stared at each other for a moment. It was refreshing. It felt like it was supposed to be. It just felt good-right!

I think we both forgot where we were for a moment before we snapped back to reality. He suddenly remembered that his daughters and I shared the same birthday, and he began to make small talk about our similarities. He even openly hoped that they would turn out to be as well-rounded as I presented myself to be. I loved the fact that he was so tuned into the Sagittarian characteristics and traits of his girls. It meant even more that he was in complete acceptance of their undeniable independence and boldness.

Jordan left the deposit and asked if he could see me after I got off work. Our dinner the night before was so wonderful, and that kiss was so heavenly, how could I say no?

He slowly walked away, and my eyes were stuck to his bowed legs like I was spellbound. I wonder if he felt like Gloria from *Waiting to Exhale*. You know the scene where she was walking away from Marvin when he was on the back of the moving truck and she says, "*I hope he's not watching me walk away! Ooh, he's looking!*"? I must've been Jordan's Marvin because he turned and gave me this cute little wave before disappearing in the sparse crowd of late evening shoppers.

It's way too early for love, but I love the feeling I have when I'm around this man. I had this goofy type grin on my face for the rest of the evening and couldn't wait for closing time.

Just as the mall announced there was fifteen minutes of shopping time left, a potential customer came in the shoppe. She looked at some of the pre-made pieces on display and inquired about specialty pieces being made asking about the average completion time for some of these pieces and how did I determine what the charge would be. She kind of sounded like competition fishing for advice more than a customer looking to purchase merchandise, but I figured if I could help her get a business off the ground or give tips to improve what she already had going, it would go in the column of helping our independent entrepreneurs grow stronger. So I gave her all the information she requested, and she ended up ordering a moderate lap throw with a simple five-letter name on it. I told her it would be ready for pick up in 17 days. Another satisfied customer!

I started humming a little tune that was kicking around in my head and pulling my displays back from the automated gates to avoid damaging the equipment.

"Five minutes 'til closing! Please complete your purchases at this time. Remember, our shopping hours are 9:00 am till 9:00 pm, Monday through Saturday and noon until 6:00 pm on Sundays. Please have a safe evening!" As soon as the automated system stopped, the metal gates started lowering at the fronts of each establishment. That was the one thing I really respected about this mall; it gave everyone equal opportunity.

Another woman approached just as the gates lowered and started with random questioning, but her tone was a tad bit forceful and bland. I was still up for helping new entrepreneurs in their endeavors, so I offered my card and tried to guide her towards contacting me at a later time. She accepted the card but kept eying me strangely like she was studying me. I thought,

'How odd was that?' but I didn't really give it another thought at that time.

      I gathered my personal items and some yarn to start on the new client's lap throw and made my way into the reserve hallway only to see the strange woman standing in the main hall of the mall just watching. I felt a little uneasy, so I waited for Tony from The Pretzel Shop to come and escort me to my car.
      She looked harmless, but in the city where I live, one can't be too careful.

# 5

I met up with my Prince Charming down at the Boardwalk in Virginia Beach for a close-to-midnight stroll under the autumn stars. The moon reflected its silvery smile off the subtle crest of waves beating gently against the shoreline, and it was breathtaking. I absolutely love the feel of moist sand as it graces the creases of my toes; it feels like a free pedicure from God. The night was warm with a cool breeze perfect for romance. Jordan was wearing a pair of blue basketball shorts and a white wife beater that looked powder blue off the ocean water and the light of the moon in the dark blue sky. He carried both sets of sandals while we were strolled hand in hand sharing childhood memories of beach adventures with our families. He came from a large family, the third of seven children, and I had no siblings, but our differences seemed to accent each other.

Jordan talked about holidays at his parents' home in Kansas. He talked of tornado season when they had to bunker down in the cellar for protection. Although their home was never taken away by any force of nature, there were always repairs to be made after each storm. Some were really major, but most were minor in comparison to some of the neighboring towns.

I learned that he grew up on a farm and loved the farm life. Fishing was his favorite outdoor activity. He named every animal they ever owned, and he loved planting potatoes more than anything else. He also shared that, because there were seven children, every seventh batch of eggs that were laid by their chickens, they spared to keep the chicken population up. His younger sister was such a fan of fresh, fried chicken that one would be crippled just about every day. A crippled bird had to be served up like a sacrifice instead of left defenseless against other chickens and intruders. It was just the humane thing to do.

I was too familiar with the farm life having grown up in the same type of environment down in the Carolinas. My favorite part of farming was cropping the plants. You get to go through a check list to see if the yield was ripe for the picking. There was coloring, size, presentation, density, and texture. The process seemed tedious to those unfamiliar, but it was second-nature to homies.

I told him how I used to eat the field peas straight out of the pods because they were so tender and sweet. He laughed a bit when I told him about my pet pig named Oink and how I would walk him through the city streets like a dog. My mom and I found and rescued Oink from a fishing embankment at Lake Mattamuskeet in Hyde County, North Carolina – one of our favorite fishing holes.

"So, you mean to tell me that you're a fisherman?" He had this look on his face like he really wanted to believe me, but there was an inkling of doubt there.

"Why? You find that hard to believe or something?"

"I just find it interesting. Maybe we can ride down to Carolina one weekend and fish. You said Lake Mattamuskeet? Sounds super country!"

"Are you teasing me, sir?"

"No, doll, just fascinated, that's all, but I know that I can out fish you any day!"

"That sounds like a challenge!"

"Oh, it is!"

"You're on!"

Just like before, Jordan was the perfect date. He was an outstanding individual, and I could feel myself falling hard and fast for this man. I had to catch myself before I pushed him away by being too fast. This was one of the nights I tucked in my memory bank to pull out just for smiles when he's not around. This was the night we shared our *first real kiss* and our first kiss; just like I said, *PERFECT*! Not too wet, but wet enough! Not too much tongue, but just enough! Jordan was a nibbler, and I loved that. He paid attention to every detail, like the way my body pressed harder to his every time he nibbled my bottom lip. So he would pull me in closer to him. He noticed how I would surrender whenever he kissed my neck, so he held onto me a little tighter.

I wanted him to hoist me up on the stairs leading up to the boardwalk so I could wrap my legs around his back and pull him so deep into me that I could taste our future. Even though the time may have *felt* right, the *timing* was all wrong. It was too soon! I wanted to lick his nipples as he howled at the moon while punishing me for making him wait this long, though. I wanted him to pound me so hard that I would be wearing the 'watch your step' sign etched at the top of each step backwards as a tramp stamp. I even wanted to get caught by some rental cop so enthralled by Jordan's technique that he would keep watch while jacking himself off to our display. I wanted so much – so soon.

The kiss seemed to last forever. It was a good forever, but I still wanted more. Our lips finally parted and our eyes danced a ballet that was both sensual and provocative. I wanted to experience every possible position revealed in the silhouette of his shades every time he blinked. I was ready to turn my ass up on the beach of the Chesapeake Bay and howl at the moon myself, but Jordan had once again shown me another perfect evening. I felt like I had struck gold, and I wasn't even digging for it. He topped it off by walking me to my car and giving a light cheek kiss before seating me and buckling me in.

"Safety first, doll!"

Before I pulled off, I promised to call him as soon as I walked in the house. The thoughts during my drive home were just as tantalizing as the kiss. I was soaked by the time I pulled into my driveway. Memories had started mingling with the daydreams and desires, and I was having problems separating the two. I created my own fantastical reality. I was lost in the dream and suddenly snapped back to reality when the front porch light popped on. I had to gather myself before I got out of the car. Maybe it was a good thing Jordan and I had spent some time sitting in the wet sand.

Just as I promised, I called Jordan as soon as I walked into the kitchen and thanked him for another wonderful evening. My next call was to my best friend, Frieda. She always wished me the best at everything I set out to do. I knew that Frieda had to meet Jordan; she was my confidant. Whatever I was too blind to see in him, she would willingly point it out for me like real friends do. Although Frieda was bi-sexual, our tastes in men were very similar, so I knew she would be honest and truthful.

We stayed on the phone for almost two hours talking about Mr. Jordan Hines and all the trouble I could see myself getting into with this Adonis. He seemed to be the total package. That was scary, exciting, refreshing, and some mo' stuff, but I was loving every moment of the ride he was taking me on.

# Jordan's River

# *6*

Frieda and I met at a job we shared as drivers for a Portsmouth cab company, Safety First Cab Company. Our birthdays were just days apart and only four years separated us in age. She was the older between us and the oldest of three among her own siblings. For a spell, I was even attracted to her brother, Frederick. He was a shit talker, and it was something about a man who could match me in wit that sparked my interest.

Frieda and I were the only two overnight female drivers, and we formed a bond because we felt the need to look out for each other. I was the quieter of the two, and I think she felt the need to protect me. I have never understood why quiet translates as weak. I was far from weak, but I appreciated the 'big sister' look-out all the same.

Being fellow Sagittarians, we constantly competed with each other out on the road. We would race to the same fare coming from opposite ends of the small city. I always thought I had the advantage because my mother was a Drivers' Ed instructor and a bit of a daredevil back in the day. I learned a great deal from her.  Sometimes, I would concede to Frieda because she was a bit of a sore loser.

She had grandchildren to work for, and I had my own children to work for.  We both had to bust our asses in that aspect of a man's field just to make it work.  We stuck it out through the robberies, attempted robberies, the attacks, and even the black-balling by our own company.  When the male dispatchers felt we were hustling too much, they would send us on ghost calls.  Or when we would shut them and their sexual advances down, they would send us to the funeral home delivery doors or the cemeteries to pick up ghosts.  For some reason, they found that quite amusing and called it payback for allowing ourselves to be captured in their snares.  Personally, I found it majorly annoying.

Frieda was a fast talker and had some other coals in the fire, so when the cab company shunned us, she had something to fall back on.  I had nothing.  I even had to give up my apartment and move back in with my mother.  When I realized that I was causing more harm than good in her house, I left my children with her and chose a life of homelessness.

Prior to working for Safety First Cab, Frieda was somewhat of an escort - a 'lady'.  She was a very attractive woman, about five feet, eight inches tall with thick shoulder-length hair worn mainly in a ponytail until she had a 'date'.  Frieda was very much a tomboy, but she looked amazingly beautiful in a dress with flawless, long legs and perfect feet.  She knew how to be seductive, without giving up the cookies, and get paid for it.

Although bisexual, Frieda knew she had a stunning figure and appeal, and used it to her full advantage.  She tried to teach me the tricks of the trade, but I harbored too much romanticism and desire. I wanted love, not a series of momentary get-bys. This lifestyle was too much like being a hooker, and I just couldn't see myself in that position.

There was a Master Chief in the United States Navy named Earl who frequently desired Frieda's company. She was the perfect eye-candy for him and his demanding style because his wife never wanted to accompany him to any of his functions. So he paid Frieda good money to be there. She just had to hang on his arm, smile, and laugh at a few corny ass military and/or war jokes. She played the part, but she never compromised herself.

Then there was George. George was different. He was her choice of men to be involved with because as long as she had known him, he had never allowed her children or grandchildren to have anything less than a huge Christmas and Easter. He wined and dined Frieda just because, but she stayed frustrated with him because he suffered from erectile dysfunction. Her wheels were turning and his were stuck in the mud. Because of her frustration, she demanded oral from him, but it became pretty clear that he really wasn't into that, so she would always said she was going to leave him alone until Earl or the others weren't quite coming through like she needed them to...then it was right back to George.

Frieda was also an escort for women in the lesbian scene. As much of an alpha as she is, she enjoyed playing the role of the eye-candy for men and women. The day of the week and the situation determined which she was most attracted to at the time. Usually the money was the ultimate deciding factor.

It was challenging for Frieda to play the role of an individual who was not opinionated. To say she was outspoken would be an understatement. She believed wholeheartedly in standing up and speaking out for what she believed in. Her favorite phrase happens to be, "I don't give a fuck what you think or say; statistically..."

She's was smart when we met, and she's a thousand times smarter now, but somewhere in the midst of dealing with George, she slipped into the drug scene. Alcohol had always been our vice with an occasional spliff, but once cocaine and crack hit the scene, I started backing off from Frieda. I never turned my back on her because I knew she needed me to keep her grounded. Hell, she was there for me when I needed her. Why would I cut out on her?

Eventually, Frieda got free, and we were right back in sisterhood. She was the one who turned me onto the job with the hospital. I was such a regular patient of the emergency department, she convinced me to apply to get the good benefits. Hell, most of my visits ended up not costing me a thing because I worked there. Then the nurses would let me stay in the empty rooms once I got up on the floor, and rest is history.

It was only natural for me to pull Frieda up with me. She was my rock in some really shaky times, and I knew I could trust her and depend on her.

When the time came for Jordan and Frieda to meet, I was more relaxed than normal. Jordan had already won my heart, and Frieda was the best sidekick a girl could have. At the dinner table, I felt like I was sitting on the side of the best team in the world.

"So, Jordan? It is Jordan, right?"

"Yes. Jordan Hines. How are you, Miss..."

"Just call me Frieda. What do you do for a living?"

"I'm a chef. I work at Locks Point out in Great Bridge. I hear you and Chris frequent there."

I knew the grilling was just getting started, so I sat back and let the fun unfold. I knew Frieda was relentless, but Jordan was extremely straight forward. That made for an interesting time. Either Jordan had absolutely nothing to hide, or he was so well rehearsed, we couldn't tell the difference. Lunch lasted well into dinner hours, and I was taking it all in like a little child.

Jordan's River

# 7

Jordan and I had become a real heavy item in a very short time. I felt like I was his 'main squeeze' because we spent so much time together. I learned so much about him and was equally willing to share a great deal of myself. He gave me a different purpose, a reason to be more, a reason to do more. I loved this man so deeply and still do.

A week after the boardwalk, Jordan made a surprise visit to the shoppe with a bouquet of daisies. How did he know these were my favorite flowers? I didn't remember ever telling him that. He told me that we were not going home that night because he had a surprise for me other than the beautiful daisies. Of course I was baffled, but I trusted him.

He had secured a hotel room in Williamsburg so I could get away from the hustle and bustle of my normal routine. When we got there, he had me to sit in the car for a few minutes while he went inside for what seemed like an eternity. I secretly hoped his reason was to prepare the room for a night of hot, sensual pleasures. I felt myself drifting into another moment of fantasy, and I had to snap out of it. The lines of desire and reality were becoming blurred once again. Maybe he was gonna fix that tonight.

He ran back out to the car and opened the door for me to make my grand exit and even grander entrance. When I walked into the room, there were lit candles everywhere, all of them leopard print (another personal favorite that I had not disclosed). They were all different shapes and sizes. Some round, some square, some short, some tall, some fat, and some skinny. The bed was lined with yellow rose petals, and there was a purple negligee' on the foot of the bed for me to put on. I excused myself and went into the bathroom to shower only to find that there was already bath water drawn for me. The temperature was perfect, and there were more romantic candles lit all around the bath. Of course, I asked him to join me, and he graciously obliged.

We slid into the tub together, and he just held me for the longest moment. Feeling his silky skin against my own allowed me a sense of freedom I had not felt in years. I felt I was right where I was supposed to be. That was the night I actually fell in love with Jordie. His compassion was of an intensity that I had only dreamed of. His warmth was infectious. His love was radiant. And, I was absorbing every bit that he sent out.

I allowed Jordie to bathe me - all of me. For the first time in years, I felt free and complete. I didn't feel like I was being compared to anyone from his past or a photo-shopped woman on the cover of Cosmopolitan. The best description of him touching me was 'good and right'. There were no outside negativities pulling at me. Maybe, the fact that he actually bathed me instead of that annoying barely rubbing soap on your partner thing new couples do made the difference. It was like he knew me or like he was bathing me the way he bathed himself or the way he wanted to be bathed. I didn't know how, but his phalanges worked magic through the lavender wash cloth. I was in my own little heaven.

After the soothing bath, he patted me dry with a towel and laced my neck, shoulders, and back with tender kisses then he led me from the bathroom to the bed where I slid into the negligee' that fit perfectly. Being a woman of thicker proportions, I did have an inkling of a moment of doubt wondering if he had selected the right size. He did, of course! His eyes revealed his true feelings – and so did his manhood. He was definitely pleased!

Donned in nothing but a hotel towel, I could see that his body was milk chocolate and smooth. His abdomen was well defined like, LL Cool J's's. He had an apple-shaped butt and a very even skin tone. No scars or blemishes marred his perfect skin, at least none that I could see. He looked absolutely scrumptious, and I was just like a kid in a lollipop factory. I had to take a lick. *Oh, boy*! What a lick it was! Get your mind out of the gutter. I was a good girl! I started at that spot on his chest right between his pects and slowly worked my way up to his Adam's apple, collecting every droplet of water the skimpy towel left behind. For my pleasure, there were quite a few. I noticed that he was keeping his hands to himself, so I released him from clutch of my tongue.

# *8*

Jordie massaged me right out of my attire with this peach-scented oil and told me more about himself. He didn't allow me to speak that often, only when he asked questions that required answers. He wanted me to keep my answers as brief as possible because he wanted me to "think as little as possible to give the mind a break". He said I work too hard and told me that "tonight (was) mine"! Then he kissed my neck just under my left ear so tenderly and lovingly that I almost lost touch with myself. I felt like I was floating. I felt the warmth of his body as he leaned in closer with each caress. The ambiance of the entire evening was so on point that it was magical. I felt like I was living a fairytale!

I flipped over exposing my full naked frontal on his demand and felt absolutely no inhibitions at all. I was free! I was his! I was complete! This was right!

"Tell me your most intimate fantasy," his tender voice blended with the soft swoons of Boyz II Men singing "I'll Make Love to You"! They were right at the part where Nathan was singing *close your eyes – make a wish – and blow out the candlelight – for tonight is just your night – we're gonna celebrate all through the ni-i-i-ight...* I settled into the warmth of his hands and let my mind roam just past that state of pre-meditation where you're still lucid, but almost hypnotized.

As corny as it would have sounded two weeks ago, it was perfect for this night. "My fantasy is an impromptu fairytale wedding. I want to arrive at an open field with only the ministers and close friends and family present with everyone dressed in all different shades of purple. There are flower girls with the pretty curls and handmade baskets throwing daisy petals as they stroll down the aisle. Two handsomely attired ring bearers are carrying two very unique wedding bands on handcrafted pillows. I want nothing like a traditional wedding."

He was taking in all I had described with such intensity and devotion marking his stern brow that it made me want to go deeper into detail. He looked like he was literally writing this all out on a mental notepad. I imagined him flipping the pages. Jordie actually listened to me, and it was a beautiful thing. What woman doesn't want to be heard?

He gently kissed the tip of my nose and held me as we slumbered together all night long. It was another perfect night with sweet, Jordan Hines. Another perfect moment! Until...

*Demons dance dangerously in the depths of my dreams*
*I drift drastically to decode the demonic deeds*
*I'm lost!*
*Although I run away, I'm drawn to the depths of his darkness*
*He dangles delights that dazzle like dreary drapery*
*I'm gone!*

Just as the dark figure of my dreams was reaching out to pull me into him, I woke up in the security of Jordan's arms. He whispered, "it's okay, Love! I'm right here! I won't let you go!"

I turned over and buried my face in his chest and cried. I thought the dreams of the past were over. I thought the memories of the homeless nights, literally fighting off the muggers, rapist, and killers were shattered fragments of a past never to resurface again. Why now? Here I am in the arms of the most wonderful man I had ever met, and they come creeping in like the stench of rotting bodies beneath the concrete floors of an old house revealing the dirty little secrets I never wanted exposed.

Of course, this opened the door to the homeless part of my past. Although I didn't consider myself hiding it, I never wanted to discuss it. It was that nasty, unpleasantness that needed to stay kept away like a disfigured cousin in a bell tower.

Jordie and I sat up for hours reliving the two and a half years of my life, introducing him to the barter system of survival, fight for position, steal for protection, sex for food, and payback for status. Those who couldn't hang in the streets got arrested trading their freedom for three hots and a cot. Those who were weak either took up with someone who was strong, or they were killed. Women were frequently raped and sodomized, and girlfriends were traded for drugs and food.

Nine hundred thirty-two days on the streets! I was a prime target for rape being a medically barren woman, but I played the game of stealing pads and tampons to give the appearance that I was on my cycle. I was safe in Portsmouth during that week. I could let the gas run low in the car and be close to my children. The rest of the month, I had to stay close to never-sleeping areas like the beach or really secluded areas like the backwoods of Holland on the other side of Suffolk. Sometimes, I would play the game so well, I could pull off the menstrual thing in different cities on different weeks.

Even with all the counting out days and perfect planning, I became victim to rape three times. The first time, I was beaten within inches of my life. That earned me eleven days in the hospital, three of which I was in a coma. The second and third times, I learned to play possum. I was as lifeless as a blow-up doll. I think these guys thrived on the fight because the second and third times lasted less than five minutes before the assailants fled.

The streets taught you lessons, and I was sharing them with Jordie. I was baring my soul to my comfort. I felt relieved!

It was hard getting back into the reality of my life after such a wonderful night with this amazing man. That evening was so poetic; it just put me in the mood for spoken word. I stepped out to Future's Wednesday's at Charles Place on Wythe Creek Road in Hampton, what we called across the water, on the peninsula. They always had the most amazing talent. It became my 'get away from it all', but tonight, it was my 'get a grip' on it all!

# *9*

After a couple of months being around Jordie and not succumbing to the pleasure of him, I was starting to have doubts about his intentions and motives with me. There were so many mixed emotions tangled in my mind. I felt like he was just trying to gas me up for the okey-doke, but I also felt like he was infected with something and was being extremely cautious about his next course of action with me. I felt he was hiding something, and I started to feel he just wasn't as attracted to me as he led me to believe. I wanted answers. I had to know something and soon. I was, literally, about to explode!

We went out to Topeka's Restaurant, and I started grilling him for answers. I asked him, very emphatically, why he had not made love to me or at least attempted to. I told him I was more concerned than anything and was starting to feel apprehensive about our relationship and his feelings for me. He assured me everything was all good and I had no need to worry about anything. He said he was crazy about me and thought I was extremely beautiful. He was just the type of guy who took his time.

"You know, Chris, you learn over time to appreciate every aspect of a woman - not just how well she can please you sexually. You learn to become a sponge to her words, her attitude, her personality, hell, her everything! I don't want to minimize anything about us for a roll in the hay, if you know what I mean."

They were all the right words; I just needed the actions to match. I mean, to some degree, they had matched up just perfectly, but I was usually the one staving off the wolves until at least a month had gone by. This time, it was him not making significant advances.

He explained to me he wanted something more meaningful than a romp in the bedroom or 'a roll in the hay'. He wanted something everlasting and permanent. I swear, I think this man stepped out of my dreams. He was just too... perfect! These are all the things I have ever wanted a man to say to me and Jordie said them with conviction and without being prompted! Yet, I still wanted him to bounce me like a rag doll atop a memory foam mattress until we confused the fibers so much that *it* forgot.

We each went our separate ways after dinner, and it allowed me time to think about everything that had transpired between us up to this point in our relationship. I knew he was more than a piece of meat, but at this point in time, I needed that piece, for my sanity.

I called Frieda when I got to the house to ask her opinion. I understood what he said, but I was still very confused. I had never actually encountered such before in any man. This was something the girls and I would normally sit around and talk about, but I really didn't want to involve too much outside help. I just wanted Frieda. I mean, I felt something was wrong with me or just out of place.

"Girl, I don't know what to do. I feel like a clogged fire hydrant waiting to be drained," I ranted!

"And right about now, you have the sense of a fire hydrant. You are just that crazy, Bitch!" Frieda's direct approach was always sobering!

Even though she frequently points out how crazy I am, I always feel better after talking to her. I was still a little unsettled about this situation, though, so I decided to take a drive just to clear my head. I just wanted to get rid of all the negative thoughts. I drove for almost an hour before I found myself pulling into Jordan's driveway. I sat in the car and contemplated whether I should get out and go to the door or just drive away. I knew I had no business being at his home unannounced even though the unspoken invitation was there. He had certainly never popped up on me like this. I hated being in this state of confusion, though.

All of these crazy thoughts were running through my head. I started reflecting on the night in Williamsburg at the hotel room, and I started yearning for him all over again. I mean, I wanted him so badly that night, and it just intensified as time went on. When I recollected my thoughts, I realized that I had actually gotten out of the car, and I was about to knock on his front door.

Jordan's River

44

# *10*

Just before I raised my hand to knock, Jordan's door opened like my presence was the key to a secret dungeon. He was standing there in all of his beautiful, dark chocolate lusciousness. "Hey, Baby! What in the world took you so long to get here?"

I stepped across the threshold, I realized that the house was set up like he knew I was gonna be there. There was mood music, candles, incense, low lights - the works. He didn't miss a single opportunity to reel me in deeper. He closed the door and locked it behind me, and I was still in my evening dress and heels, but for a very short time. I am still a little unclear as to how he disrobed me so quickly and effortlessly. I think the threads must have actually just melted away as my attire ended up around my ankles.

Standing naked before him, he gently kissed every inch of me, and I do mean every inch. I became a wet noodle before him. Jordie lifted me, without straining, onto his favorite captain's chair. His kisses were just enough to drive me over the edge, but he replaced his tongue with a middle finger in my hungry mouth as he delighted himself with my dime-sized nipples. I almost exploded! Then he stopped. I mean, all activity ceased. *Everything!* Talk about being confused! I think livid is a better word for what I was feeling at that moment. What was he thinking? Was he even thinking?! I was definitely taken aback but still kind of in a euphoric state. What the hell was he doing to me? I didn't know how to respond to his tactics.

Just as I was about to speak out on the lack of events occurring, he ordered me to close my eyes. Without hesitation, I complied like a child that had just been lovingly corrected by a parent. He blindfolded me with what felt like a silk scarf, and all I felt was something cool and moist gently caressing my lips. It smelled like a strawberry. Then, I could feel the texture of the seeds as they danced over my hungry lips. I parted my lips and tasted the sweetest fruit. We shared a few more strawberries, some dipped in chocolate and some not, but all were shared mouth to mouth. His lips would slightly graze mine with the last bite of each strawberry. This was the only way to indulge in pre-sexually shared fruits!

His hands again massaged my 'G' cups and he left signature kissed along my abdomen before gracefully tasting the fruits of my intimacy. I had longed for this from the very first moment I laid eyes on his gorgeous, full lips and saw the motion of his tongue when he spoke. Jordie was definitely on top of his game. Just the right touch with the tip of his tongue in just the right spot caused me to arch my back and lace his teasing tongue with the nectar of my approval. I literally felt the earth move, and my body flowed with its rhythm as my orgasmic waves crashed against his lowered mandible.

Before I was allowed to completely gather myself, we moved in unison to the plush carpet where he slowly entered his throbbing pleasure pole into my waiting chamber and made love to a sistah like no man had ever done before. I felt each vein, each ridge, and every single pulse, every everything! His lovemaking was just as smooth as his skin. His style was as demanding as he was, and I relished every moment of it.

This was well worth the wait. I was hooked, and he knew it. Just as he was about to share his passion juice with me, he yelled the most astounding words. He yelled, "You are my queen"! He then flooded me with his sweet passion.

He was right; I was his queen. He was definitely ruling my kingdom that night!

We collapsed into the plushness of the carpet in exhaustion and cherished the lustful moments we had just shared. Like I said, he was well worth the wait, but I don't think I could have waited any longer than I did. I knew that I had found my happiness and that there would never be another after that. He had definitely set a new standard forever!

# *11*

There was something about poetry that just seemed so right after a night of Jordan, so I took a flight to New York to sit in at the Nuyorican Poetry Café on East 3rd Street. As I walked in the door, the host (Rhythm and Rhymes affectionately known as RnR) gave me a wink and called up the feature performer for the evening. This cute, full-figured chick was there all the way from Portsmouth, Virginia, just like me. RnR introduced her as Sexee Kittee.

There was this confident and commanding presence about her that just lured the crowd in. Her words were so full of life. She was committed to the arts, and it showed.

*"Here! Take my hand!*
*Let me lead you into forever*
*Where love grows at a tempo faster than weeds*
*Where tears flow into rivers starting from the trickles of laughter*
*Where words sound like carefully selected rhythm and blues*
*Dedicated just to you from my soul*
*Where the folds of my arms become pillows to your weary head*

*Lay with me*
*Control my open note with your staff*
*Tangle me neatly in your limbs*
*Whisper your intentions as we print notes of various values*
*In the sheets*
*Call it - sheet music*
*You treble – I bass*
*Forcing me to FACE the fact that Every Good Boy Does Fine*
*As we play our selection in perfect time*
*Let us dream*
*Playing repeats in a drifting concerto*
*From legato to staccato, then presto, we're at rest*
*Sharing sweet memories of prior moments*
*Until the radio glares reminders of life outside of our touch*

*Have a good day, Baby!"*

Her piece brought to mind the night Jordie and I had just shared, and she spoke with such power and authority. She demanded the audience's attention as she followed her poem with a brief introduction of herself. Apparently, this woman had been writing poetry since she was seven years old, but she had only recently started doing spoken word. She claimed to be nervous, but she sounded cool, calm, and collected to me. As much as I enjoyed spoken word in our area, I was surprised I had never heard of her. She was definitely one I needed to follow.

She explained she also had aspirations at one point of being an emcee, and she got the crowd up on their feet and hyped when she broke out with this rap piece,

*"My business*

*It's my busine-e-e-ess*
*My business, you need to get your own..."*

Evidently, many of them had heard it before because the majority of them were singing right along with her. I have to admit, her flow was tight, and she was captivating, but my mind kept dipping in and out, reminiscing about the night before with Jordan. I couldn't believe this man was so perfect in every way. He said the right things, did the right things, made all the right moves, and now he had me under his spell.

I cut out of the venue before the show was over and took an early flight back home. I did, however, manage to cop a copy of Sexee Kittee's CD so I had something to listen to on the flight back. I was bobbing my head to the beat and humming a little loud when I noticed the teenager of the only other family in first class staring at me intently. I gave a light smile, closed my eyes, and started singing...

*"My business*
*It's my busine-e-e-ess*
*My business*
*You need to get your own..."*

"Ladies and gentlemen, the runway seems to be a little crowded this evening so we will be circling a bit before we land. This shouldn't take too long. I hope you've otherwise enjoyed your flight!"

The landing was so smooth, I didn't even wake up. The same teenager that was staring at me gently shook my shoulder.

"Miss? You're listening to Sexee Kittee, right? You should listen to Typical Man Syndrome, track number 4. It's kind of funny, but it's good. My mom even likes it. I mean, I like her whole CD, but that one and the one you were listening to earlier are my favorites."

"So, she's pretty popular, huh?"

"Well, they don't play her on the radio or anything, but she does a lot of house parties and local venues. I think she does more spoken word than anything now, but I like her music."

"I'll have to check that out definitely.! Thank you for the heads up!"

"No problema!"

On the walk to the car, I thought, "*why would I want to listen to anything about a typical man? I've got anything but a typical man!*" But when I got in the car, I popped the cd in and selected track 4 like I had been programmed or something.

*I don't want you no more*
*But you can't seem to let me go*
*Weren't you the one who cheated?*
*Weren't you the one who mistreated -*
*Me - I now see it all so clearly*
*Baby - Let's not make this harder than it has to be*

*(You've got that typical – typical man syndrome*
*You're acting like a fool,*
*And I don't know what I'm gonna do with you*
*That typical – typical man syndrome*
*You'd better leave me alone*
*Little boy, you'd better go on back home)*

*I'm sick and tired*
*Of the changes that you put me through*
*You think you've got me puzzled –*

*You think that you've got me confused*
*But I realize that to you, love is just a game*
*Let me tell you something, my feelings just aren't the same*
*You'd better go*
*Go on, boy, got outta my face*
*Cause I ain't got time for playing*
*It's time to put you in your place*
*You'd better go*
*Go on back where you belong*
*I think it's time for you, my baby*
*To go on home*

As I pulled into the driveway, the chorus came back around again, and I could totally identify!

*You're always forgetting the little things I ask of you*
*Like our anniversary, you forgot my birthday, too*
*But it's okay 'cause materialism ain't my way*
*Please understand, though, that I can't ask you to stay*
*You gotta go*
*Cause this ain't the right time for us*
*So pack your bags and get to steppin'*
*And hop your ass on the next bus*
*You'd better go*
*Cause I can't take this anymore*
*So gone and get your things together*
*And hit the door*

*(You've got that typical – typical man syndrome*
*You're acting like a fool,*
*And I don't know what I'm gonna do with you*
*That typical – typical man syndrome*

Jordan's River

*You'd better leave me alone*
*Little boy, you'd better go on back home*
*That typical – typical man syndrome*
*That typical – typical man syndrome*
*That typical – typical man syndrome*
*That typical-a-al – typical man syndrome*
*yeah)*

How I wished I had had access to that song in my past. I was sitting in the car just letting the tunes resonate. I thought of at least three of my exes who fit the description of a man suffering from TMS. I wished I could go back in time just long enough to drop this on them or, at best, wished they were somewhere listening to it now.

When I walked in the front door, a slight chuckle escaped my lips putting me in the position to be questioned. When I explained to my daughter what was causing the laughter, she joined in the singing and we trotted off to bed.

# *12*

Breakfast was just as divine as it smelled the next morning. Jenique really did a fantastic job on it. She stuck her big toe all up in it. Man! She even warmed the syrup just like I like it. I was never a big fan of pancakes or waffles, but this morning, the waffles, sausage, grits and eggs were beyond perfect, even down to the little pat of butter and pepper atop the grits. This child of mine is excellent therapy for me. I know exactly why God gifted her to me. She's my cushion, my strength, my sounding board, my friend, and my rock!

We washed and dried dishes together and talked about school. Jenique was very sweet and very misunderstood by a lot of people. Her way was not, by any means, traditional. She just demanded her own space and refused to allow intruders to take that from her. So, if you violated that space, be prepared for the fallout! All decisions have consequences. Invade her space, suffer the wrath. She was also Sagittarius, my mini-me!

After a delightful breakfast, the phone rang, and I anxiously ran to answer it. It was Jordie on the other end, "Baby, open the door!"

When I opened the door dressed in nothing but a Tinkerbell bathrobe and Dallas Cowboys slippers, there were two delivery trucks waiting outside. Each was clad with a massive amount of daisies and balloons. The deliverymen kept bringing them in. I had never seen so many flowers inside one place in my entire life that was not a funeral home or a church conducting a funeral service. This had never happened to me before! This man was actually wooing me. I had never been wooed before, but I sure loved this feeling. Of course, he was nowhere in sight, so I hurriedly took my shower and got dressed in my gold and black Roca Wear sweat suit, black and gold Timberlands, and black Starter cap.

I was definitely planning to thank Mr. Hines in person for his thoughtfulness. While preparing to go, I was rehearsing my words in the mirror, and even rehearsing *his* responses. Yes, I was having that conversation. Don't act like you haven't done it, too. Fess up! You know you have!

I would wait for him to open the door, jump in his waiting arms, and plant this huge kiss on him. Then I would thank him mostly with batting eyes, and he would say, "Anything for you, my darling queen!" Then I would say, "You are too good to me!" and kiss him again. All of this played out in my head while I twirled around the living room full of daisies and admired the beauty like – Tinkerbell - only without the wings!

I even had the fleeting thought of going to the Lexus dealership and just buying him a car to replace the faded blue Honda Civic he sported, but I thought that would be way too superficial. He needed something totally unexpected and well-deserved. He needed something more personal.

I had it! I knew exactly what to do and he would really love what I had in mind. This was destined to be the gift of all gifts, for sure!

Soon after dressing, there was a knock at the door. Jenique yelled for me, and I scampered down the stairs only to be serenaded by a singing telegram asking me out on an afternoon cruise aboard the Spirit of Norfolk, one of Hampton Roads' most frequented attractions. Now, you know I would be a fool not to accept after all the beautiful flowers and an invitation of such epic proportions. I felt like a teenager all over again, and I loved it!

Well, it was back to the drawing board with the outfit. I had to change clothes all over again! We had a cruise on the *Spirit of Norfolk*? Yes! I changed into blue slacks with a flirty sky blue, low, v-cut, knit sweater. I knew that there would be dancing aboard vessel because my mother had gone several times before with my children, so I put on my dancing shoes. Hahaha! My navy blue Naturalizer pumps donned with a cute little gold bow went perfectly with the gold accessories I had in my natural hair. I was not one for a lot of jewelry; I only wore my trusty, gold-trimmed Timex.

Before I left the house, I had to make his life wonderful. I called Melanie, his ex-wife, and asked her if the girls could spend Christmas with us. She and I had talked a few times before, so it was no surprise for her to hear me making such a dynamic request. She asked for time to think about it and promised to get back to me later on that night. That would be so perfect for Jordie. He really deserves this. That would say 'thank you' much better than words or a car, for that matter, ever could. He deserved something real and genuine for his efforts.

Jordan's River

# *13*

Of all the things that I had done, especially since coming into so much money, this was the first time I would ever step foot on the Spirit of Norfolk Tour Cruise Ship, and it was thrilling. I could not believe that I had not made this happen for myself in all these years. This man had rented the entire liner for a private cruise, and I was so totally unaware. When I boarded, I saw all of our closest friends and family, Melanie, her husband, Marcus and the girls. I even got to meet his siblings – all six of them, and each seemed to approve his selection. I was on top of the world.

I felt like a queen. Jordie had gone all out for me, and I knew that I was truly blessed with a good man this time. I wasn't gonna do anything to mess it up.

There was a whole table laid out with fruits, cheeses and crackers for appetizers. We had smoked salmon with garlic sauce and a squeeze of lemon, dirty rice, and grilled green beans for dinner. Then there was dessert - a beautiful miniature carrot cake baked and iced to perfection just for me. Another item from my list of favorites that I had not disclosed, but Jordan had definitely done his homework. The band was even playing my favorite song, "*Forever In My Heart*" by CeCe Peniston. The music softened as Jordie rose to his feet and invited me to the dance floor. How could I say no? Everything was beautiful and set for dancing. He was graceful and sharp, and I was too willing to follow his lead. I had not danced like that in three years. The last time was with my son's teacher at a parent/teacher special conference honoring all honor roll students.

I remember smiling a lot. I remember wanting to whisper sweet nothings in his ear, but I didn't want to miss one note the wonderful band was playing. I just wanted to absorb everything. While we sashayed across the floor and found ourselves positioned directly in front of the band, the dancehall diva, herself, stepped out from the shadows and started singing. I was floored as I tried to lessen that gaping hole between my nose and my chin. I can definitely say I was pleasantly amazed and shocked. Jordie whisked me all over the dance floor as Ms. Peniston sang, and everyone around us gawked.

We did this elaborate spin and dip, and I was totally comfortable as Jordie continued to display his dancehall moves and stunning skills. As we made our way back to the middle of the floor where there was an "X" that truly marked the spot, his daughters, Princess and Duchess, came out with a beautifully wrapped box slightly smaller than a shoebox. Puzzled does not begin to describe my vivid expression. Princess held the box while Duchess opened it revealing the most beautiful tiara you could ever imagine. It was all sparkly and shiny, and you know that girls love that kind of bling!

My mother then walked over and placed it on my head as if to symbolize her approval of the gift *and* the man who gave it.

Then she took my right hand in her left and his left hand in her right and put our hands together like we were preparing for another dance or something. She was just as crazy about this man as I, and that meant the world to me. Any man that was accepted by my mother, (and he was the only one) had to be the one.

Mom scooted to the side just enough to free up room for Jordon to come and stand directly in front of me. He knelt down, sheepishly looked up at me and asked for my hand in marriage. I was so choked up all I could do was nod my yes. The words were caught somewhere between exhilaration, excitement and joy.

Laticia, Marco, and Jenique then came out with a garment bag, a shoebox, and a ring box respectively. This man had thought of everything! Laticia and Frieda had picked out the gown, and Marco and Jenique got the shoes. I only opened the small, beautifully designed gift box. Inside was the most beautiful two-carat heart-cut diamond mounted in a 24-karat gold setting. Stunning? No! Phenomenal!

All I had to do was set the date and show up. How hard was that? I mean, there were just six weeks left till Christmas. I could not think of a better time to gift myself to such a deserving man and receive such a wonderful gift of love in return.

My real fairytale was beginning!

Jordan's River

# *14*

When I got back home from such a reeling evening, the phone was ringing. I couldn't wait to answer it because I was so sure it was Jordan, but it was Melanie instead. She was the first person, outside of the party, to congratulate me on our engagement. She also declined the holiday visit knowing Jordie and I would probably be honeymooning at that time. There was no bad blood between us, and that just made the entire situation better and more relaxing for everyone, especially Princess and Duchess. But it wasn't bad for Jordie and me either.

I walked around for the next two weeks with my head in the clouds and my mind in a daze. I was showing off my ring to everyone I came in contact with. Then I started feeling guilty. I had not yet revealed to Jordan who I really was, the fact that I owned seven Centers and was the sole proprietor of the crochet shoppe. I knew I had to be the one to tell him, and this had to be revealed before we became man and wife. I really didn't want to begin a united life together being deceptive, and I knew in the depth of my soul that he would understand. I also didn't want him to walk into this type of lifestyle so totally unprepared. There would be press, there was security; there were so many things that would permanently change for him.

Jordie had been out of town for almost two weeks trying to finalize the wedding plans on his end. I had planned to talk to him as soon as I got out of the shoppe later that night. Fortunately, he called later in the evening to let me know that he got back in town a little earlier than anticipated and couldn't wait to see me. He was truly my Boo!

I had finished the girls' afghans and was ready to present them to Jordie. These two pieces of art were definitely among my best works. I figured what better way to present the afghans than with the great revelation of who I really am. It's not like I was a different person, just what I was actually worth. I felt so convicted; I absolutely had to let him know right now! Our relationship and the success of our marriage depended totally on my honesty at this point.

The last hour of work was kind of slow, so I decided to write my king a fitting poem.

*Love comes in all forms, shapes, and fashions*
*Love brings many emotions including passion*
*I fell in love with you for the beauty you possess within*
*Your beauty without was so fine, it was pure sin*
*No doubt, I lusted after you, but you showed me something more*
*Your mind, your spirit, your compassion, I grew to adore*
*You turned me on to something I have needed for so long*
*A man who was physically, emotionally, and spiritually strong*
*I guess after all is said and done and the day has come to an end*
*I can say that in you I truly have a friend*
*I know that friends come in degrees like rounds to a ladder*

*But you are the best; with you, my insecurities don't matter*
*You treat me like I want and need to be treated*
*You've shown me a different type of love that I've needed*
*I can say that I have learned to open up a little bit more*
*Now I am open to what the next moment might have in store*
*I thank you for the moments and the time that we will spend*
*I thank you so deeply for really and truly being a friend*

      Pleased with my work, I folded it over and placed it under the register for safe keeping. I felt like I had invoked Miss Sexee Kittee. The words were genuine and heartfelt. I figured sometime close our wedding day would be the appropriate time to share this piece with him.

Jordan's River

# *15*

I decided to hold off on the revealing of my past until the next evening. I still had a few things to tie up at home, and I had not spent a great deal of time with the kids since Jordan came into my life, so a family night at Dave and Buster's in Georgia seemed perfect. It was a twenty-four hour spot that we all enjoyed, and the hospitality was definitely welcomed at this point. This way, I could pick their brains and see how they really felt about Jordie. Everyone already approved, but I wanted to know how they really felt. I needed to know if they had any fears or inhibitions.

I called ahead to reserve the seats for the four of us, and assured everything was all set. When we were situated in our seats, we were told that there had been a change of plans. Our flight was actually going to New York. For a moment, I panicked until Jordan peeped through the curtain and said he had a surprise for all of us. I guess there was no need to grill the kids. The only way he could have known about my plans was that they called him. After all, my answer was standing right there wrapped in the burgundy divider curtain.

The kids seemed overjoyed to see him, so I knew they contacted him. I guess any fears I had they weren't receptive were diminished. I can't deny that I was happy to see him as well. I knew that I still had to have *that* talk, but with the kids around, this was definitely not the time.

When we landed in New York, Jenique may as well have taken flight all over again. I didn't worry too much because we were from Portsmouth, Virginia, so having street smarts was an absolute must. She was off and running. The Big Apple always fascinated her. I don't know if it was the fast pace, the lights, or just the different atmosphere, but there was something about this place that called to her, and she didn't hold back. Laticia was always sucked into the musicals on Broadway, but honestly, she was sucked into the musicals anywhere for that matter. She had a passion for math and music, and Marco was all about the restaurants and the beautiful women. He claimed he would find his wife in New York when he was ready to get married.

There was something about Time Square that just screamed LIFE! Maybe it was the fact that no matter how dark it actually was, all the bright lights made it look like daytime. No flash was required when taking photos, no flashlights were needed for items dropped or misplaced in the bottom of your purse if you carried a purse. You just had twenty-four hours of life lights, flashing and blinking and neon and almost-feels-like UV rays lights!

After taking in all the lights, Jordan had made reservations at The Dallas Barbecue restaurant. It was busy and fast-paced, but the overall ambiance was amazing. It had this elegant but country feel to it. Imagine that, in the city! You kind of felt like you might run into a celebrity, but it was really laid back and comfortable. The food was delicious! There was one main difference about the north. There was no such thing as free refills on the drinks. Even water came with a fee attached, but that's the price you pay in the Big Apple. Though money was not the issue, I was still mindful of spending. You can't stay well-off being reckless.

Jordan asked to order for everyone because he wanted to show just how much he had come to know us. He knew that Jenique had nothing to do with pork, and I loved salads. He knew that Leticia tried to stay away from fried foods and with Marco, it was no holds barred. He did an excellent job! He and I ended up sharing a thick-cut sirloin.

Jenique had barbecued wings and fries. Leticia had salad and baked chicken. Marco had a combination platter that seemed have little bits of heaven all over it. It was all divine – the meal and the company. The evening was definitely made memorable.

After dinner, we did a little sight-seeing before going back to the airport to fly home. I fell asleep on Jordie's shoulder, and it was some of the best sleep I had ever had. It just didn't last long enough!

Back on the home front, I decided to grab a few hours of sleep before going into the shoppe. I knew the center was functioning well, and this was a slow time of year because most families were generous enough to pull their loved ones in, so the homeless population wasn't so high around the holiday season. I missed the rat-race, but I enjoyed the calm. It gave me time to shop and prepare for the holidays for family and friends.

There was still this nagging intensity to tell Jordie exactly who I was and what I did, so I once again decided to give him a visit just to sit down and put all the cards on the table. I figured we might even go to Locks Pointe and share a meal. I thought a meal on the deck overlooking the water would be ideal, and I still had not given him the blankets for the girls. The excitement of the look in his eyes was fueling me to get the evening done even faster!

# *16*

After securing the shop, I was on my way to Jordie's house. I had to remind myself there was a speed limit because I was driving out of control as I whipped around curves and weaved in and out of traffic. I wanted to fly to him. I wanted to blink like a genie and be standing right in front of him with the soul-bearing news so that we could move forward without any inhibitions. I wanted it done. Every fiber of my being was telling me that he would understand and even agree with my methodology.

When I got there, I parked in his driveway and gathered everything to take in the house. My goal was to make only one trip. As I got closer to the porch, I heard the interrogation from the restaurant the night I questioned Jordie about why he had not made a move to advance our relationship sexually. I knew it was a recording because it was me talking, but I was outside, and my voice was coming from inside. Why would he record our conversation? I really didn't understand what was going on. Was he studying me? Was he studying *us*? Was this his method of remembering important things? Why wouldn't he tell me that we were being recorded? What was going on?

I decided to knock instead of using the key given to me. I felt like he might need that time to turn off the recorder or just get it together period. To my surprise, some strange woman answered his door. I was sure I had never seen her before, but she looked familiar. She was close to my height, maybe an inch or two taller, and looked to weigh a solid 200. She was beautiful, and yes, I did size her up.

"May I help you?" She snorted when she snatched the door opened.

"Um, yes! My name is Chris. I'm Jordan's fiancée. Is he in?"

She laughed like a crazy woman, but I wasn't finding the situation amusing at all. Who was this trick? Why was she answering Jordan's door? Why was he not answering his own door? Where the hell was he anyway? What the fuck was going on?

I had met all of his siblings and their families just a couple of weeks ago, and this was not one of his sisters or sisters-in-law.

"Nobody by that name is here, lady!" This time she added a bit more attitude

"Ma'am? I'm sorry, but I know I have the right house! I mean, I *am* engaged to the man! Just who are you?"

"Look, I told you ain't nobody here by that name, so get the fuck outta my doorway and carry your ass!"

I paused! I had to get it together. Maybe it was the 'street' in me that made me want to whoop her ass, but maturity said walk away. I didn't know what the hell was going on, but I listened to maturity, and slowly backed away from this low life standing in Jordie's doorway. I knew not to turn my back on this stranger. That's a rule of survival I learned from watching the Saturday morning Kung-Fu movies growing up.

Frustrated and confused, I left. I drove with tears in my eyes for about an hour, and I didn't want to go home and have Jenique see my face like this. She was so protective of me, she would have made her way over there and handled all of that. I went to Frieda's house instead. This thot's candy apple face was so fucking familiar it was perplexing.

"Aw, Baby! What happened?" Frieda held me in her arms like I needed Jordie to do, and she stroked my tussled locks out of my eyes kissing my forehead.

I knew Frieda was bisexual and always looking for the chance or an opportunity to squeeze her way in. Although this was not the time for her opportunity, I *needed* my friend. The one person I needed to make sense of this was... What the hell was he? Who the hell was he? I mean what the fuck?

I told Frieda everything, from my reason for going over, to my Terminator 'I'll be back' retreat. My instinct was still pulling me towards the gun cabinet in Frieda's home that housed my .357 IMI Desert Eagle, which I called 'Git Right'!

Having money had its perks, of course. I kept Git Right at Frieda's house because I knew my hair-line temper only needed a twinge to make my trigger finger twitch. I always had my Jennings 9mm tucked safely away at the house and kept my little Colt Banker's Special on me most of the time. Jordie expressed his concern with me carrying a piece very early in our relationship, so it had become habit to remove it from my personage and leave it in the car before being around him. This is why the burnt Rice Krispy sloth that answered Jordie's door was still alive, I thought.

All Frieda could think about was going back to confront this heifer, pulling out the heavy artillery and getting to the root of the problem, if you know what I mean. At this point, all I wanted to do was cry myself to sleep somewhere and wake up from this horrible nightmare! Frieda called my daughter to let her know that I was in good hands and not to worry. Jenique would figure that I had been out drinking or Frieda and I were in deep conversation. Spending the night at her place was nothing new or alarming to either family. As long as I let the fam know that I was alright, it was all good.

      I had my own room at Frieda's house. It was my private little get away. I crawled into my queen-sized Tempur-Pedic and drifted away into la-la land, but I kept seeing images of this woman, her mad laugh. She was taunting me in my dreams. There was something so familiar about her. Where the hell did I know her from?

# *17*

I must have called Jordan's cell phone at least ten more times only to get no answer. The answering machine wouldn't even pick up anymore. Messages I left ranged from concern to confusion to complete frustration and anger. I didn't sleep well because I was so frustrated! My tears soaked my pillow making me feel like I was drowning. Here it was, twelve hours later, and I *still* had not heard anything from him. Knowing I had no tolerance for bullshit, I knew it would not be in my best interest to go back over to the house without talking to Jordan first. A confrontation with this woman would definitely mean eminent death, and I didn't need that on my hands or my conscience, for that matter.

After my morning coffee with Frieda, I rushed home to see if Jordan had left any kind of a message. No such luck. I felt my world spinning out of control. I had no business confronting this woman again in my current state of mind, so I did some local running around to keep my mind occupied.

While I was in line at the post office, I kept being haunted by the image of this woman and my intuition kept telling me that her face was too fucking familiar. My phone rang, and it was Jordan's number. I stepped out of line quickly and answered it straight away. It wasn't Jordan, though! It was that woman. She had the audacity to interrogate me, shooting questions like she was 5-o. "Who are you? How long have you known this man you call Jordan? Do you know him by any other name? Is this your method of contact? Why won't you answer me?"

In my mind, my answer was, "Bitch, I don't know you, don't want to know you and don't care to answer any of your fucking questions. I just want my Jordie!" None of these words came out, though. Only liquid sadness rolled from the corners of my eyes, spilling anger and disdain onto the concrete floor of the lobby of the post office. I felt enraged, and that was not good. I was already on medication for hypertension and depression. I could think of nothing else but beating the brakes off of this skank ho or bustin' a cap in her pathetic ass! I realized that I was shaking uncontrollably, so I went out to my car to try and get myself together.

I still had business to conduct, and I couldn't let my personal life come between the realities and responsibilities of my professional world right now. I was about to erect an eighth building down at the waterfront in Virginia Beach, and the architect I wanted for the job lived in Massachusetts. Joseph Mitford and I worked together to design the Suffolk complex, and I had been teetering out of my comfort zone with such a large project as that one. I wanted this particular facility to be even larger, maybe twice the size as the Suffolk one. All I could do was consult with someone who had experience and knowledge of buildings of this magnitude. This facility would hold up to 650 residents and have a more expansive transportation unit, so this baby had to be his project. There would be two cafeterias and more accessible rooms for handicapped residents. I trusted Mr. Mitford. Sounds funny that I would trust any man at this point, given my track record with men, but Joseph and I only dealt on a professional level, so it was easy to trust him at his work.

I took the time to redirect my focus, clear my anger, and went back into the post office to send the request for service and ideas of the Virginia Beach – Lackner Center, Two. While standing in line, I just could not shake the vision of this woman's eerily familiar face. It was like she was looking down on me, or watching me. She was haunting me!

My fairy tale was literally falling apart, bit by bit and piece by piece! I had to keep reminding myself to keep it together for myself, my family, and my businesses. I hated to position I was in!

# *18*

Two more days went by and still no word from Jordan. I was getting no real help from the authorities either. After forty-eight hours, I was able to list him as a missing person, and Melanie backed me up on that. We tried to play it cool in front of the kids because we didn't want them to worry, and had to watch how we carried ourselves because our engagement had become high profile in our cities. That part was my fault for having money and clout in the area. I couldn't make a move without someone knowing who I was and trying to find out what was going on in my life.

I took it upon myself to check everywhere that I knew him to hang out, to no avail. He was a workaholic like me, so there weren't too many places to check. I kept his disappearance as silent as possible because a media circus was not the kind of publicity we needed right now.

Because I had had such a lousy track record with men, I couldn't handle any pity, jeering, or consolation from anyone, especially not now. I found myself quickly drifting into the mode of work and home, work and home. Frieda was waiting for the word from me to go and off this chick and be done with this Mickey Mouse bullshit. But, I never have been the type to fight over a man, and ultimately, that's what it seemed this situation was panning out to be. My main concern in all this mess was simply to know that Jordan was okay. I just wanted him to be safe.

As upset as I was with the entire situation, I still very much loved Jordan, and that couldn't be denied. I was still dreaming of him every night. He was still consuming my every thought. I just needed to see him, talk to him, get some sort of explanation as to what the hell was going on. My emotions were all over the place. I decided to take a day or two off from the Center and just gather my thoughts.

I went down to the waterfront to think. Water was always the best therapeutic medicine for me. It always seemed to have this silent, rhythmic flow that my mind found a way to blend with; I called it aquavibing! I would lose myself in the melody of the little ripples created by the passing ferry or tour boats. Each passage would play a different tune. Sometimes, I would catch myself humming a siren-like tune to match the rhythm of the waves.

As I strolled along the boardwalk, I almost bumped into this out of place looking couple. At second glance, I realized it was Jordan and the psycho chick that answered his door the other night. His back was to me, but she saw me coming. I walked right up on them in all of my boldness and tapped Jordan on the shoulder.

As he snapped around, I could see that he had been in some sort of altercation and was pretty beaten up. There were numerous cuts and bruises, his left eye was swollen almost shut, and his clothes were tattered and torn. He looked like he had been run over by a Mack truck. I wanted to demand an explanation, but my anger momentarily shifted to fear...not only for him, but for myself as well. Who did this to him? I mean Jordan was a mild-mannered man and really didn't bother or provoke anyone. He worked hard and spent most of his down time with me and the kids. Occasionally, he'd go play basketball with the fellas, but they were upstanding guys. I couldn't imagine any of them having any type of beef with him. What the hell was this bitch doing here?

He looked at me like I was a stranger and said, "May I help you, ma'am?"

"What the fuck?" You know, Jordan, I hate that 'ma'am' shit! And why are you acting like you don't know who the fuck I am?"

"Ma'am, are we in your way? Do you need to get by?" He asked as he shuffled slightly to his left.

"Jordie! What the hell is wrong with you? Where have you been? I've been calling and leaving messages. I have even gone to the police for help. Are you okay? Do you even remember me? Do you have amnesia or something?" I reached out to him as I asked the latter questions.

During my barrage of questions, this bitch was yelling all kinds of crap in the background. I was so focused on Jordan, I had tuned her completely out. She made sure she came through.

"Why is she calling you Jordie? Who...the fuck...is... Jordie? Somebody's gonna tell me something!"

I was happy to see Jordan, scared out of my wits that he looked so bad, and pissed off with this whining bitch all at the same time. So, I punched her in the mouth, just to shut her the fuck up. I had to eliminate part of the problem just so that I could think a little more clearly.

While she was nursing her busted lip, Jordan gave me this funny look and said, "Ma'am, I'm not who you think I am. I don't know of a Jordie. Please leave; this is not a safe place for you to be right now, especially alone!" He lurched like something had stabbed him in his side and kept looking like others were around. He just kept doing this funny thing with his eyes, looking scared out of his mind. By then, I added overly-heightened suspicion to the array of emotions I was already feeling, a concoction which was nearing the boiling point and about to explode.

Why was he acting like this? What the fuck was going on? This was definitely the Jordan Hines that I knew and loved. He had the same eyes (well, eye), same voice, and same tat with the name of his girls. He knows me. I can see it in his eyes. What is he protecting me from? Or is it even me that he's protecting? What does this bitch have to do with all of this? And who the fuck is?

Before the heifer could completely recoup, I shook my head, wiped my brow and considered going back to my car for my Colt. It was broad daylight, and my common sense kept telling me that I didn't need the extra heat. Something had to give!

# *19*

I knew in the back of my mind that the time had come to go for back-up. I was at my wits' end, and something had to be done to get to the bottom of this. Whatever *this* was! I wasn't going out like this and didn't care how bad my track record was with men. Something in my core was telling me that Jordan was worth fighting for, and I had to follow through with that feeling. I really didn't wanna lose the best man I had ever met. So, yeah, I was ready to fight tooth and nail to get my man back. I had all the fuel and ammunition needed, literally, to get rid of this bitch for once and for all. I just had to be smart about it. Like I said, having money had its advantages.

I thought about it long and hard. I knew that she had not done anything to me, personally, but for her to act like nothing had happened to Jordan, with him being battered and cut up like that was absolutely deplorable. She was shattering my world. I couldn't shake the image of him, the tattered clothes, the swelling of the eye; you can't tell me that he deserved this on any level!

I made a straight path to Frieda's house and, of course, my girl was down for action. It was always good having a thug bitch in your back pocket. Whenever shit needed to be done, you had everything you needed. Frieda was my, well, everything! She was born in money, but was the black sheep of her family. Her parents never cared for her outspoken honesty. She had that Sagittarian knack for telling it like it was, so she was shunned early in life. Her brother and sister were spoiled like royalty, getting anything mum and dad thought they might want, while Frieda, the oldest, was pretty much left to fend for herself.

She became sister to the streets at the tender age of sixteen and pulled away at the age of 17 when a back-alley rape left the assailant dead and Frieda pregnant. She was proof that doing the right thing is *not* always the right thing to do. A trip to the Portsmouth Police Department to report the crime proved that true as well. Frieda Lynn Washington was the victim, fighting for her life. The evidence from the rape kit was not used in court at all. Only after she served six years of a life without parole sentence was the kit brought up and Frieda finally exonerated. Forced to deliver her first born behind bars, she had to turn her over to the system straight away. But, "Virginia is for lovers", right? They keep saying that bullshit!!

*A young mother*
*Barred at the age of sixteen from her home*
*Left out in the cold – the streets to roam*
*Forced in the family way by way of rape*
*A shank in a cold dark alley was her means of escape*
*How quickly she would learn*
*How the hands of justice turn*
*Forced to bring life forth behind bars*

*Issuing the newborn daughter her first set of internal scars*
*Feeding her into the system without haste*
*Her outcome, unpredictable in this oh too common case*
*Mother confined - Daughter unsigned*
*Now we find they're both trapped behind*
*Bars!*
*Separated by a system that vows to protect and serve*
*In a state where you rarely get what you deserve*
*That good ol' Virginny commonwealth*
*Where you gotta be much more than common to be wealthy*
*Where skills and knowledge are not judged fairly*
*Where the bottom of the food chain workers get paid barely*
*Where well-to-do, stuck up parents refuse to carry*
*Their own*
*Where free choices of meals come sorely*
*Because too many of us live so poorly*
*Beneath the poverty line is where we reside*
*Yet that line is not wide enough to hide*
*Our despair*
*Those who vow to protect and serve would rather tuck us away*
*While the hard-break-your-back workers have double tax to pay*
*And the state tries to convince you that you deserve your stay*
*Because of your good and honest deeds*
*If those who deserved freedom were freed*
*Maybe we wouldn't need*
*So many of these*
*Bars!*

When I walked into Frieda's, the entire mood was somber. On television, the Chesapeake Police Department, Sheriff's Department, S.W.A.T. Squad, and ATF were in a standoff in Jordan's neighborhood. Whoever this person was had taken a woman and her children hostage and was threatening to kill them all, starting with the youngest, if the authorities did not back off. I recognized the house. It was only three houses away from Jordan's. I was ready to kick into stealth mode and try to get to him.

My first instinct was to pick up the phone and call him, but I knew that wasn't a wise move. So, I stayed glued to the screen and watched intently for anything that might show that Jordan was okay. I mean, I felt for the family, but they had the help they needed to come through this. Where were the police when Jordan's eye was getting swollen? Where were the police when he was getting cut up? Where were the good old cops and all of their help when I needed them to find out what was going on? My faith was withering at a rapid pace.

I kept watching and thinking, hoping that Jordan was not tied up in this somehow. I was praying that he was okay. Then, the phone rang, and somehow, I knew that it was for me.

"Hello! Yeah! Who is this?"

I could tell Frieda was getting agitated, so I lightly wrestled the phone from her and answered, "Hello, this is Chris!"

"Baby, I need you to meet me somewhere. I promise I'll explain everything when I see you. You name the place and the time, and I'll be there. Please, Chris, just give me this chance!"

"Have you lost your motherfucking mind? What kind of game are you trying to play with me, Jordan Hines? I don't believe you and all this bullshit!"

"Chris, please," he pleaded! "I know I can make everything up to you if you just give me this chance. Trust me!"

"Trust you? *Trust you*? Are you fucking serious? You want me to trust you after all of this? I don't even know why I'm on..."

"CHRIS!" He interrupted my banter and made me jump. "Look, woman. I know this is fucked up. I know this better than anyone. Please, just name the place and the time, and I promise you I'll be there. This needs to be done face to face."

I could hear the quivering in his voice. "Jordan, are you telling me..."

"Chris, Baby, place and time, please!"

"Sleepy Hole Park. You know the spot. Twenty minutes!"

I slammed down the phone and gave Frieda a look. She knew that I had to go, and I had to go alone. I picked up my Git Right, snapped it into my holster and walked out the door. Oh, it was about to be on! I had no more tolerance for bullshit and no more time for shenanigans.

Jordan's River

# *20*

It was only fifteen minutes from Frieda's driveway to the Park. I needed that personal time to get to our spot. It seemed like the longest fifteen-minute drive in history with everything that was going on. Caught by every light and behind at least two cars at each stop sign, I made it there with plenty of time to spare. I walked through, what I called, the Tarzan trees with the long swinging vines attached to them (I never knew what they were really called), made my way over the clearing, and reached the small patch of woods just on the outskirts of the park at the far western end. It was *really* secluded. With the exception of the occasional passing of the Park Ranger, no one ever frequented that spot. As a matter of fact, Jordan and I found it by accident and had actually taken the time to clear it out ourselves. That's why we called it our spot.

I sat on the little, wrought iron bench that faced a fountain overgrown with vines which had this beautiful rusty cherub spewing water into the waiting bowl. This place was so remote there weren't any coins in the fountain. I glanced at my watch, saw that I had two minutes to spare, and took a few deep breaths and exhaled slowly to calm my nerves.

Jordan slowly approached me from behind like he wasn't sure how I was going to receive him. I wanted to spit fire in his face and slap the taste out of his mouth. But all I could do was throw myself in his arms. I missed him so much. I loved him! As angry as I was, when I saw him, all of that melted away.

"Chris, baby, I'm so sorry for everything! When I saw you on the boardwalk earlier, I wanted nothing more than to grab you and hold you close to me. This shit is so crazy, I don't even where to begin!"

With my head still buried in his chest and through tear stained cheeks, I said, "How about at the fucking beginning, asshole?" I had never called Jordan anything like that before, but it was so relieving due to the circumstances.

"Let's sit down. This may take a while!" He led me over to the little bench.

He still had on sweat the pants with the cuts in them, and I couldn't help but notice the bandage peeping through one of the holes. I gasped and reached for it, but he grabbed my hands and assured me that he was okay.

"Chris, I'm gonna need you to just listen. This isn't gonna be easy for me. Just listen and bear with me, please; but hear me completely out!"

"Jordan, you're doing a whole lot of talking and saying nothing. Just say it. I'll shut up! I promise!"

"The woman, if you can call her that, who answered my door, is Candace Anderson. I met her three months after Melanie and I broke up. Hell, I was lonely and impatient. Fuck that, let's call it what it was. I was horny and weak. Candace came along and promised me 'happy'!"

He let out a little chuckle and continued, "I should have taken the time to get to know her. I fucked up. I opened my home up to her. I opened my heart to her. I opened my life up to her. Hell, I opened myself up to her. She painted this picture of being the perfect little lady, until I had to work late one Friday night and forgot to tell her that I was picking the girls up on my way home.

"I was supposed to get off at five, and I didn't leave the restaurant until eight, so by the time I picked up the twins and made it home, it was almost ten. Candace flipped, *in front of my girls*. She was freakin' spazzing out. I attempted to gather the girls' things and take them back home because she threatened harm to them! You know how I feel about my babies. I refused to let my girls see me lay hands on this woman, though. I wanted nothing more than to lay her ass out right there in my living room floor, but I held back. I think she felt invincible at that point. I don't know if she was used to dealing with thugs, but I'm not that guy. She was working really hard at pulling *that guy* out of me that night! I also think she felt that the demise of *us* was inevitable during her little rampage!"

All I could do was look at Jordan. "So, I still don't get it!"

"Baby, trust me, you will! Do you remember about five years ago, this woman set two houses in Hampton on fire with the people still inside one of them, a woman and her twin girls and..."

"...her lover owned the other house. Yes, I remember that! She was locked up, wasn't she?" I had to interrupt.

"Yeah! That was Candace's handy work. The burns on Princess' leg...?"

"Oh, my God! I had no idea, but..."

"I know! The *lover's* name was Mario, Mario Antoine Naples as reported by the news."

"But..."

"Shh! I had to change my name, Baby. She's crazy was only given ten years for attempted murder. I know how manipulative she is. I know how dangerous she is, and I didn't want her to ever find me. Hell, she's the reason I've stayed single this long. I refused the witness protection program because I had heard of too many horror stories. The last thing I wanted was to be another statistic in that kind of system.

"She threatened and tortured me psychologically for weeks after the evening she showed her ass in front of the girls, even while she was behind bars. I never could tell Melanie why the girls couldn't come over to the house any more. I didn't want them exposed to her or her craziness."

I stared at him like he was the most dramatic episode of my favorite soap opera. There was still so much more that needed to be explained.

# *21*

Jordan filled me in on intricate details of his short lived life with Candace, and I listened intently trying to hold my questions until the very end. I still did not understanding why he couldn't tell me what was going on before now. He had plenty of opportunities. I was becoming enraged.

"Chris, I didn't know that Candace had followed me when I took the girls back home. She was quick to let me know she knew where they lived, and she threatened to kill them. Those are my babies. I felt like she had me by the balls."

He reached down and took my hands and disclosed that he found out that Candace had been released the day after he proposed. I lost control at that point. Something in me just disconnected!

"But we talked on the phone every night, Jordan, I mean, Mario. What the hell am I supposed to call you? Why couldn't you tell me about it when you found out? Why did you have to go to the extreme of changing your name? Is she THAT possessive? I understand about the witness protection program and all, but really? And if you really felt like we were in danger, you would have made a way, Jor...Mari...Damnit, Luigi!"

"YES! And some! She IS crazy! She IS possessive! She's out of her mind, for real. Possessive is an understatement! I changed my name for safety reasons. Marcus and Melanie got married in Italy on a private beach for safety reasons. When they got back to the states, they were really low-key for a while, but Melanie got tired of the sneaking around.

"Ultimately, we all felt that Candace would be after me, so I came up with Jordan Hines. I had a dog named Jordan that died in the fire, and my mother's maiden name is Hines. She never knew about my mother's name or the fact that she's still living, and she never bothered to learn the name of my dog. I slipped up and got comfortable with her, and I'm still paying the price for that slip up."

"Oh, God, Jordan, you had a baby by her!!!"

"God, no! I'm paying for that slip in up in the fact that I am still ducking, dodging, and was hiding from her. Now, that I've met the woman of my dreams, the love of my life, and Candace has resurfaced, I feel like all of this, all of us are in jeopardy!" Jordan began to tremble a bit.

"How was I supposed to bring this up before? When we met in the grocery store, was that supposed to be my opening line? Or the night in the hotel would have been the perfect opportunity, or even the night we made love. Chris? Really?!"

"Like there were no other times, Jordan? We've had dinners, outings, dates, happenstance meetings - you've had numerous opportunities. You knew she was out, and that alone posed a threat to you and everyone around you, that includes me and my family!" I had no intentions of letting him feel any sympathy from me.

"I left town to tie up the loose ends of the wedding, but I also wanted to insure that Candace wouldn't be a threat to any of us, here. I love you, Chris, and our united family means too much to me to let anything happen to any of you!" Jordan grabbed my hands and held onto them as if they were his lifeline.

Pulling away, I got up and slowly walked over to the fountain. I wished I had a handful of coins to toss in just for the sake of answering the zillions of questions floating around in my head.

"Chris, Baby? What are you thinking, baby?"

"I'm thinking I don't know you. I'm thinking the Jordan I thought I knew would have told me this and we could have tackled this together. I'm thinking you really...."

"You know, you have some nerve, lady. Miss worth billions. Miss owner of seven Outreach Centers and about to erect an eighth. Miss owner of Kitteez Kreationz. But I understood, Chris. You wanted to know I was for real, and I have been right here. But, you still have not said a word about any of that shit to me. When did you plan to tell me; when we were old and grey sitting in rockers on the front porch of your castle? Or were you planning on keeping that as your private little girlie secret?"

"Jordan, don't you dare try to compare the two situations. Nothing about my life has or ever will put yours or the lives of your daughters, Melanie or Marcus in danger, or the rest of the family for that matter! You knew she was released. You knew she had a deadly fixation on you. You knew she was your fatal attraction and the moment you accepted me in your life everything about me was in danger. You jeopardized my entire everything, from my family to my business to you! Look at what's at stake here. Then tell me how they compare!" I could not believe he was trying to make this about my silence. The nerve of him!

"Chris..."

"No! I was with you. I was all for you. I let you in. I may not have told you what I had, but I never did hide anything from you, either. Yeah, I wanted to make sure this was real. Truth be told, I showed up at your house that night to tell you everything, but that crazy ass, possessed, demon-bitch answered your door and started trippin'! Yeah, she threw me off my game. She had me all discombobulated, but if you had opened up to me about this wellness-threatening shit you got going on from the beginning, maybe, just maybe, my money or my worth could have made it all go away. We are...were supposed to be in this together. We, you and I, were an US, a unit, ONE. We tackle shit together, not apart! I thought you knew that I'm not one of these weak, ass little bitches that would just cower at the first sign of..."

Before I could finish, he ripped the leg of his sweats and tore his shirt off to show the fresh cuts on his body. "She was in my house when I got back. How do you think I got these cuts? From HER! See these marks around my wrists? I got those about twenty minutes after I called to let you know I came back early." He looked exasperated at this point.

I was floored! I was speechless! But as much as I wanted to hold him, I was still hurt and angry. I felt betrayed.

"Chris, listen! I had just gone in to take a nap before you came, baby, and my whole everything changed. I knew you were coming, so why would I purposely put myself in this type of unscrupulous position?

"Baby, I was gagged and tied up, Chris. That's why I couldn't yell out to you when you came to the door. At the boardwalk, did you notice how close up on me she was? She had a gun on me, and she was threatening to shoot you! Do you have any idea how bad I was hurting, how much I wanted to hold you? Hell, do you know how much I wanted to choke the life outta that...that...THAT BITCH?

"Yes, I danced like a puppet on a string to appease her. I would never let anything happen to you or our family! And when you punched the shit out her, my insides died because I thought she was gonna kill you. I had to play her game to keep you safe! Baby, look at me! Chris, baby, please..."

I stared off into the water spewing from the lips of the cherubs like I was waiting for it to voice the words I felt. Then I opened my mouth and said, "I can't! You don't get it! Jord..., Mari...hell, you, you didn't have to be a puppet on a string; all you had to do was tell me. I would have made mountains move and even disappear for you. I would have rearranged her life for you, but you didn't have faith in me. Did you?"

Walking away from Jordan was worse than my last two weeks of being homeless. The sense of loneliness and dread flooded in like a tsunami. I felt like the existence of the past several months had been sucked out of my soul like sewer pipes sucking bath water through a drain. It hurt badly!

Jordan's River

# 22

My head was reeling, my heart was pounding, and my eyes were clouded and swollen. I knew the kids did not need to see me like this, but I couldn't stay away from them. I had to know that they were okay. This crazy shit-for-brains bitch was out here somewhere, and my all was in danger.

On the way home, I called my cabin-hand and asked that he ready the cabin for me and kids to come out to Blacksburg, immediately. That was definitely one of the perks of being rich. You could disappear whenever you needed to, wherever you needed to.

I went straight to the house and told the kids to pack. They knew not to question me and went straight to work. Marco called his father who kept my Excursion on lockdown until I needed it, Laticia called her boyfriend to let him know to put the "they're on vacation" plan into effect, and Jenique made sure everyone had all the essentials. We always packed light just carrying our own toiletries and personal electronics, especially if we had to move fast.

I called Frieda, and she made plans to move into my house immediately. I called my main center in Portsmouth and told my assistant I had to lay low for a few days, so she knew exactly what to do. She had someone in place to take over the shop for as long as I needed it manned. I knew that having money meant I had to be responsible and protected. I made sure I had written, understood, and physical insurance policies all over the place.

Although we were packed and ready within an hour, I decided to make that late night move. It's easier to track followers. There was commotion outside, so I checked the security cameras. I saw a suspicious person lingering around my car and memories started flooding in like a busted dam.

I *knew* I knew this chick. I felt like she was so close in the post office because an outdated photo of her graced the wall of the FBI's 25 Most Wanted...stamped with "APPREHENDED"; this was the *same* chick that stopped by my shoppe asking me all sorts of irrelevant questions about my business after hours. How could that be if she was released after we got engaged? Unless...

Nah; it couldn't be. That would mean that she was out and in town, and he only found out after we were engaged. Or, he knew all this time and never told me. Or, oh hell...

She had to be out because he and I had been recorded at the restaurant the night I confronted him about his lack of interest.

I suddenly snapped out of my whirlwind when I heard glass shatter. My windshield was busted. This bitch slashed two of my tires!

I called Brandon, the kids' father, and told him to meet us at the secret place, told him what was going on, who to contact and what to tell them. I warned Frieda to wait a couple of days before coming to the house and to leave my spare keys in my car parked at her house.

Whoever this was in my driveway only disabled one car. I had plenty! I didn't flaunt it because I knew there were always haters.

Brandon texted to let me know his E T A. The kids and I escaped through a lower level passage I had installed in the house when it was built. Whomever was demolishing my car was trying to gain access into my home. I knew it had to be Candace. When I thought she was some business person trying to learn the ins and outs, I gave her my address. Now I had to focus on getting my family free and clear of this mess.

We met Brandon at the point of connection, and I sent the kids in the Excursion with the specific instructions of going to get their grandmother and heading to the cabin, no other stops along the way. Brandon was to take me to Frieda's to pick up my car. I was going to get to the cabin a little later, after I finished my unfinished business. I had to see Jordan before I did anything else. I still had questions. The timelines weren't matching up. I needed truths. My truth was that I was still very much in love with this man, and that was worth the fight!

But, as with everything in my life, there was a change of plans...

# *23*

Frieda called and insisted that I ride with Brandon and the kids over to her house immediately instead of waiting around for my ride to come through. Not only was she worried about my safety with this crazy trying to break into my house, but she was adamant about me being aware of something that was going on in real time. So I made the decision to go straight to her house and send the kids off from there.

Brandon dropped me off at Frieda's side garage door and continued on with the previously set plans. I rushed in to learn that the northeast section of Camelot was blocked off by the local police, the F. B. I. and S. W. A. T. I recognized a few of the houses that were shown on television, rushed out Frieda's house, hopped in my car, and headed to Jordan's right away. Although his house was not one of the ones shown, I still had to be sure.

I did a slow roll through Jordan's neighborhood not only because I had to have the answers now, but I had to know that he was okay, based on what I had seen on TV. I didn't take the time to see what was going on or who was involved. My concern was making sure that Jordan was still alive. And, I wanted him to know the damage his secrecy had caused. He had to know what was going on at my house simultaneously, and if his answers were half-way on point or respectable, I was gonna insist that come away with us to safety.

As I got closer, I noticed Jordan and Candace standing in the driveway arguing. How did she get to his house so fast? I was lost. She was just at my house trying to tear into my front door with a sledge hammer and some other pick axe kind of tool. I know it was her because the security camera got a clear shot of her face - the same face plastered on the wall at the post office - the same face that was in mine at my shop asking me a thousand and one questions about my business - the same face that was standing behind Jordan on the boardwalk with a gun pointed at *me*. But now she was here, in Jordan's driveway, yelling and waving a gun about like a mad woman.

I was completely oblivious to the commotion that was going on just a few houses away from Jordan's. The entire cul-de-sac was blocked off, but I still maneuvered around emergency vehicles to get to my destination. I guess the intensity of the stand-off made the yelling going on at Jordie's insignificant. All that could be heard was the growling of the trucks and rescue units, the commands being shouted out over the bull horns, and people shouting instructions for others to stay inside and stay down.

I slammed on brakes in front of Jordan's house and jumped out of the car with my nine in hand and a backup clip in my pocket. I had my aim locked at her mastoid bone, and I gave Jordan this look hoping that he would understand it to mean duck and roll. I couldn't believe that I was smack dab in the middle of some James Bond type shit in Chesapeake, Virginia – right beside the damned police. I had a gun on a chick who had a gun on someone else. My heart was racing out of control.

There was silence. We were all motionless until I did that Roger Murtaugh neck role from Lethal Weapon, and three shots rang out...

Everything went dim for a moment and flashed right back in. I saw Jordan on the ground and Candace standing over him with a stupefied look on her face. Then she dropped. Did I shoot her? Did I miss her and shoot Jordan? Did she shoot Jordan?

I blacked out again.

My heart couldn't take too much of this, and before I realized it, the police were there along with rescue. I tried to stay conscious long enough to figure out what the hell was going on. All I could remember was that Jordan was on the ground and Candace fell. But, Candace was at my house. Why was I being hoisted into an ambulance?

Jordan's River

# *24*

"Miss Lackner, I'm Lieutenant Bangor. If you're up to it, I need to ask you a few questions. First of all, how are you feeling?"

I had to clear my throat before any words would come out. "I...I feel like...um...I feel sordid. What's happening? Is Jordan okay? I saw him on the ground. Candace, what happened to her?" I was so confused  All these partial thoughts were racing through my head.

"Well, that's kind of what I came to ask you, Miss Lackner."

"Is Jordan okay? Where is he?"

All sorts of tubing and cords seemed to pour from my body like external veins. There were restraints around my ankles and wrists. Everything was visible but hazy. I was confused but lucid enough to know that I had to know what was happening with Jordan. I needed answers, and this copper man was shooting questions at me like he was prepping me for a college exam. "Sir, I don't mean to be rude, but I need to know where my fiancé is."

At that moment, a nurse and another woman in a business suit walked in. "Nurse, Jordan Hines, is he here?"

"Yes, he is, Miss Lackner. He's right outside, and he can't wait to see you, but this lady says that she's your lawyer and she..."

"Miss Lackner? Miss Crystal Lackner? I'm Tanya Streets, your attorney. Lieutenant Bangor, you may direct your questions to me from this point. As a matter of fact, I need time to consult with my client. Will you please excuse us?!"

Bangor, with a look of anguish mixed with beaten exasperation, promised that he would be back later in the day to talk with me and my attorney. I knew what it was all about; I just didn't know *what* it was *all* about. I lay there replaying the last weeks that I remembered and tried with everything in me to figure out how, why, and when I ended up here in Battlefield General Hospital. "Ms. Streets, will you please tell me what I'm doing here?"

"First of all, Ms. Lackner, may I call you Crystal?"

"By all means, do!"

"I want you to start by telling me everything that you remember. Every minute detail is important, so don't leave out anything. Remember that I am *not* the enemy. I'm working for you, not against, so I need you to be completely honest with me. Deal?"

"You've got it, Ms...."

"Tee, just call me Tee!"

"First of all, I'm the proprietor of the Lackner Housing Units located throughout Hampton Roads, and I tend to really be selective with the people I meet and bring into my personal circle. Not too long ago, I met Jordan Hines at Giant Open Air Market in P-Town. It was a whirlwind romance and we recently became engaged. The thing is, I didn't tell him that I was the owner, and I wanted full disclosure before we got married. You know how it is? You want to lay all your cards on the table so there are no surprises down the road.

"I went over to his house to let him know what was going on, and when I got there, there was this woman pointing a gun at him. Everything after that gets really fuzzy. I..."

In the middle of my trying to recollect, Tee cut me off again. "Are you in the habit of traveling with a piece?"

"Tee, with my worth and being a single parent, yes - yes, I am! I live a legal lifestyle, but that doesn't exclude people with illegal mindsets trying to take advantage. I have to protect us. Bodyguards everywhere I go, especially in this small town, make me more conspicuous and an easier target than just not calling major attention to oneself." I was becoming agitated at this point!

"Chris, I don't want you to push yourself, so calm down, please! Thank you for telling me what you've told me, but I need you to be completely honest with me about everything. That's the only way I'll be able to properly defend you. Ms. Anderson was killed, but we're still trying to figure out who did it, why she shot you, and why your...", she was abruptly interrupted.

"Hey, baby!" Jordan said as he burst into the room. I have to admit that I was ecstatic to see Jordie, and I wanted to jump out of bed and wrap all of me around him, but I could only raise my right arm, which was probably best because he was still on the mend from the abuse he had suffered from Candace's hand prior. I had been shot in my upper left chest missing my artery by millimeters. Candace wanted me dead; that was for sure!

"Jordan, I am so sorry. I came over to fight for what I believe in my heart was mine. I had no idea this crazy woman was, well, *that* crazy! I mean, I know what you told me, but I thought it was just a major obsession. This chick was on some Fatal Attraction shit for real, though, like Glenn Close boiling the damned rabbit in your house femme fatale shit!"

"Chris, baby, everything's okay! Our focus now is getting you better and out of here." Jordan's voice was calming. He assured me that my healing was the focus.

Tanya shifted in her seat before butting in. "Chris, I'm gonna leave for now, but I will return tomorrow morning after breakfast. Hopefully, I'll get here before the Lieutenant does, but in the event that I don't, you are to tell him that he has to wait for me. Under no circumstances are you to talk to him without me. Am I making myself clear?"

"Loud, and clear, ma'am!" I reached out to shake her hand and thank her for her diligence and for agreeing to take my case. As she walked out of the room, my eyes filled with tears because I really could not remember what had happened. Did I shoot and kill Candace? Why did I remember three gun shots but not pulling the trigger? Had Jordan be shot? Did Jordan have a gun?

# *25*

Jordan stood by the side of my bed like he was my personal body guard. I was still under the influence of some pretty high-powered medication, so I was in and out of lucidity. But, I still wanted him to crawl into bed with me and help with my healing in that special loving way, but I also wanted to know.., to remember what had happened the night before.

"Jordan, what happened last night? And please be completely honest with me!"

"Chris, are you going to question everything I say and do from now on? I know I messed up in not telling you about the Candace situation, but I've been open and honest with you about everything else. I just didn't want to bring added bullsh..."

"Jordan, I really don't remember what happened last night!"

"Baby", Jordan injected, "first of all, you've been in here for four days now. You've been heavily sedated because of the swelling on your brain. One bullet lodged in your chest, barely missing your heart and artery, and another grazed the right side of your head, baby. But there was just enough impact that it caused stress on the brain. We thought we were gonna lose you! Frieda's here, Melonie and Marcus are here, and Marcos is running the Center for you. He has really stepped up. He's quite a young man you have there."

"But you were on the ground, Jordan; I saw you! How did she manage to get two rounds off if I shot her first? Or did I shoot her after? I don't even remember pulling the fucking trigger. I just want to know what happened. They've got me in these restraints but not handcuffs, and I don't understand why. Am I being charged with murder? I mean, no one has even mentioned that. Please, Jordan, I just need to know! What the hell is going on? None of this is making any sense to me. Jordan, I'm starting to feel like things are spinning out of control!"

"Baby, please calm down. You're still in a very fragile state. *You* did not shoot Candace."

"But, I had my gun, Jordie!"

"And you are not to say anything to anybody about that. Do you understand me? Nothing!"

"Jordan?"

"Chris, trust me on this. Your gun and holster were removed and replaced in your car. Your gun was not fired at all, so it didn't need to be on the scene." He had the sternest face I had ever seen on him. He was almost nose to nose with me. I didn't feel threatened, but I knew in my heart of hearts he meant every, single word that he was saying to me. "I heard the third gunshot and waited until everything died down before I cleared everything. I called 9-1-1 and ran back to be by your side. That's when things got really twisted and I was cold cocked in the back of the head by somebody. I didn't pass out, but I stayed on the ground trying to see who it was, but all I could see was that it was a woman. She came out of nowhere."

There was something in Jordan's eyes telling me that this time, he was being completely honest, so I didn't feel the need to question him any further. I didn't understand why I couldn't say anything about my gun, though. As I listened to my Bae explain the events of that evening, I realized that whoever this female was had busted the window to my truck and took my belongings. She had my gun and holster, personal papers and my pocketbook, but Jordan assured me that he stopped all of my cards, and reported everything that was missing right away.

As pleasant as it was being back with my Jordie, that night was strange filled with strange dreams. My knight in shining armor had posted up in the chair right beside my bed and warded away all the monsters that popped up in my dreams until 3:34am. I bolted up like a lightning strike!

"JORDIE, SHE WAS AT MY HOUSE AT THE SAME TIME!"

I remembered this chick was trying to bust into my home. I thought it was Candace until I got to Jordan's house and realized that Candace had him at gunpoint in the driveway.

"Chris, baby, what are you saying?"

"Candace was at my house trying to break in at the same time she was in your driveway. I know that's not possible, but that was the reason I was driving the truck. She smashed the windows to my car. It's all on the security camera. When I left the house, she was still there wrecking my shit. She didn't even know we were gone. We carefully left through the trap door, and she was still trying to get in! We loading up at the end of the block, we could still see her, so, how is that possible? How was she there and *there* at the same time? Unless..."

"Chris, stop it! There is no way God would have put two evil entities on this earth, let alone, at the same time. There has to be a logical explanation. I just can't figure out what it is."

"Baby, trust me! I know who and what I saw. I saw Candace! It was her! She was in my driveway fucking up my shit and using the same sledge hammer she was using on my garage doors trying to smash the damn windows to my house. We have to tell Tee! I know I've been on some pretty heavy shit for the past few days, but I am not crazy!"

"Chris, I know you're not crazy, but what you're saying right now is not really logical. I dated this woman, and she never said anything about a twin sister. I just can't imagine that she would, she could...", he hesitated.

"See there! You don't know for sure. You already said you didn't know her for very long and things progressed very quickly. Jordan, I know it sounds strange, but hear me out! PLEASE!

"A few months ago, a woman came in asking me a bunch of questions about the shop. Thinking she may be an up and coming entrepreneur, I gave her my card because I was about to close. Another woman had come in just before her with the same inquiries. I thought it strange, but I dismissed it. But, baby, it was thought-worthy enough for me to keep her face in the back of my mind. "

"Every time I saw Candace, it was like an annoying itch that every time you try to scratch it, you can never really find the source. You know what I mean?"

Jordan's eyes were fixed on mine soaking in every word. I knew he wanted to believe my theory, but he was a man, and he had his manly doubts.

We talked a little more about the situation before trailing off into how our life as one was going to be together. I could tell that I really wasn't getting anywhere with him. I was back with my Jordan, and it felt really good to be his once again.

Jordan's River

# *26*

There was a light tap on my hospital door.

"Miss Lackner? Bangor, here! Do you feel up to answering a few questions for me this morning?"

"I don't mean to be rude, Lt. Bangor, but not without my lawyer present, sir." I tried to be as polite as possible.

Just as the words rolled from my lips, Tanya walked in and greeted Bangor very professionally, then directed her attention to me. Jordie leaned over and kissed me on the forehead and excused himself to go get coffee for us.

The questioning session only lasted a few minutes because every one of Bangor's questions was met with a "don't answer that" by my lawyer. I think Bangor got a little frustrated before deciding to pack it up for the day, again with the promise of returning tomorrow. Tee kind of gave him that I-got-your-ass look before he closed the door. Just to make sure he had gone on about his business, she went to the door behind him, opened it and watched him lankily marched toward the elevator. He brushed shoulders with Jordan on his way who took it all in stride and came into my room.

Tee sat on the foot of my bed and directed me to keep my focus on her and asked Jordan to please refrain from interfering. We needed to get this process done so I could get back to healing. It was hard to keep my focus on Tee because I was not really sure of anything that happened after I was shot. Hell, I didn't even know that I had been shot until Jordan told me while I was lying in this damned hospital bed. But, I have to admit, Tee made the whole process very relaxing and easy; well, as easy as it could be.

I was exhausted after she left, but Jordie and I shared coffee and breakfast and talked more about our fairytale wedding. I tried to slip in questions about this mystery woman, but he always redirected my efforts. His main concern was my healing and getting me in a better place. We even talked about the possibility of relocating to another state. My family's roots are here. I also had my centers and my shoppe to worry about. I mean, all would run smoothly in my absence, but there was nothing like hands on for me.

Jordie saw my passion and didn't allow me to worry any further.

I stayed in the hospital for another week with daily visits from the lieutenant only to brush him off until Tee was ready for me to talk. She was right there every morning keeping me in the loop of where we were with everything, which was nowhere.

The day I was discharged, I was unsure as to where I was going. I tried to convince Jordie to come with me up to the mountains for awhile, but he knew that our family and friends would want to be close to me. I let him pick the place, as long as it wasn't my house or his. He did good. He got us an entire floor at the Renaissance Hotel in downtown Portsmouth. We had body guards, conditional room service, and everyone had their own room. He flooded the kids with electronics. We had special privilege to the pool during closed hours, and the kids were chauffeured to school every day in a different car.

Any shopping I needed was done by someone else or online. I had to either disguise myself in order to leave the building or resign myself to staying put. I walked the hall for exercise or waited until 3:00 am to beat it out in the fitness room. I swam laps every day, but it didn't compare to the few times I was able to go out and sit on the boardwalk or ride down to the beach and put my toes in the water. The beach meant body guards. No one would see me and Jordie together knowing that deranged chick was still out there somewhere.

We talked more about this mystery woman, but Jordan was giving up nothing. Tee made sure I knew where the case stood and assured me that I was never in any danger of being charged with a crime. Jordan told me not to tell her about him removing the gun, but there were still so many unanswered questions of my own. I know they were relying on hard evidence, but I wanted blood. I wished Candace could've been brought back from the dead and killed by the wheels of justice for the shit she put Jordan through, for shooting me, for causing my family to stress, and for causing harm to the twins; for *everything* her crazy ass did. Her twin needed to pay for this shit, too, and I was certain there was a twin. As a matter of fact, someone needed to find that bitch.

Mom had become quite acclimated to her new living arrangements as long as she was able to go to church one Sunday a month and travel with her best friend to the casino every now and again. The kids were great with the idea of this whole set up for the majority of the time, but started getting a little cabin fever closer to the two month mark. I just wanted to get back to regular life or what regular life had become.

One evening at the pool, Jenique approached me crying. She said she knew who shot Candace.

# *27*

Two months after the shooting, Tee called me to her office with news. The Detectives found and arrested Candra Anderson. So it turns out Candace really *did* have a twin sister, and this poor excuse of a female was just as ruthless as Candace. I couldn't believe *no one* would listen to me! I was floored, but I was happy that I wouldn't have to stay cooped up in that damned hotel much longer.

Of course, Tee wanted me to stay put until investigators were sure there were no more family members, significant others, or other friends trying to cause us harm. Apparently, these two had left a string of bodies all across the country with their twinning shenanigans. Hopefully, with one now being dead and the other incarcerated, their crime spree was over.

It didn't take too long for the court sessions to begin. We all knew from the beginning it was going to be a long, drawn out proceeding because of the complexity of the case. If we were dealing with one crazy woman obsessed with one man and only did one stupid thing, that would be one thing. But we were dealing with two crazy women obsessed with one man, and they did multiple horrible things to so many people to have him.

Before Jordan, or Mario, even met Candace, he was engaged. His fiancée called off the wedding and never talked to him again, and he never understood why. Candace impatiently waited for Mario to get over his grieving before she slid in to take up where Shanya left off.

She showered him with all the things he thought he was missing in Shayna's absence, but, in all honesty, it was too soon for him to even assess his own needs. He wasn't even ready for a simple booty call let alone a long term sleep over.

Tee called me in for a final round of questioning. "Chris, I need you to tell me everything from the time you first encountered Candra up until you waking up in the hospital. Please don't leave anything out. I can't help you if I don't know, so even if there are things you think may be a bit shady. Let me be the judge of that. You are not the murderer, and there is no way you can be implemented, but we have to know how much we can get her with."

"Tee, can you tell *me* what happened? I'm getting too many different accounts of what actually went down. I just want to know. I mean, I really don't feel like I can tell you what I don't know!"

"All I want you to do, Chris, is tell me what you remember - everything that you remember. This case is like a five thousand piece puzzle, and there are about two hundred pieces missing. I need those pieces. You have those pieces! We can't serve justice without *those pieces*!"

I saw a tear in the corner of her eye while she was pleaded with me. I don't know who hired her to be my attorney, but I'm so happy they got *her*! She is definitely about her shit.

"Tee, just let me rest up a bit. We're supposed to making the final move back into the house today, and I'm tired. I've been folding and packing stuff away and playing supervisor to these knuckleheads all day. I just want to unwind a bit."

The truth was, I wanted to talk to Jordan about the gun business. He told me not to tell anyone that I even had a gun on me, but I know that there was a police report filed about the gun being stolen from the car because I had been questioned about it. I wanted to tell Tee everything, but I didn't want any kickback on Jordan.

As soon as I got to the house, I called my mother and the kids to go out for dinner. I figured it would be good for all of us to get out of confinement. I told mom to wear something fancy. I felt like being a little eccentric.

I pulled up in the Limo to pick up mom, and the kids met us at the pizza joint. It was all in fun; and I just wanted us to break the monotony of being shut up in the hotel for so long. Acting like kids, eating finger foods, playing games, and just having good old family fun would definitely do the trick.

The first chance mom got to pull me aside, she asked if I had talked to Jenique while we were at the hotel. All I could tell her was that my daughter came to me in the pool area crying about knowing who shot Candace. But things got kind of hectic after that, and I never really had a chance to get back to it.

"You need to talk to your baby, Baby! Don't pressure her. She needs to just talk it out." Mom had this way of talking with her eyes if her words weren't enough, and her eyes were saying this was urgent.

"Mom, in your honest opinion, should I talk Jenique before or after I talk to my lawyer? This woman almost acts like a mind-reader, and I don't want her picking up on something

I'm not ready for her to know. Mom, do you know something?"

"Talk to your baby, Chris!"

We ended the night with all sorts of goofy prizes, loads of pizza, and mad fun. Laticia opted to spend the night with her grandmother because she loved limousines, so I rode with Marco and Jenique back to the house. I held Jenique's hand and asked her if she wanted to talk about anything, and she nodded her head 'yes', but said I needed to talk to Jordan first.

I felt like a stupid pinball being bounced back and forth from person to person, and it was annoying. It was old, and I wanted answers more now than ever before, but I maintained my cool because the last thing anyone needed right now was someone going off the deep end. They were *all* pushing me there very quickly!

# *28*

I pulled the curtains open to let the sunlight in knowing today was going to be long and arduous. I scampered downstairs to surprise Jenique with breakfast, only to be met by Jenique, Jordan and Tee already waiting for me. Jordan met me in the doorway and guided me over to a chair to be seated.

"What's going on, hun?"

"Dooms Day!" Tee said with the straightest face I seen her with yet. "I need you to come clean about everything."

A quick phone call to Jordan the night before let me know that I could tell her about my gun being in the car but not on my person - there was no need.

I took a deep breath, held Jenique with my left hand and Jordan with my right and started telling Tee the entire chain of events as they poured out into our lives.

"The woman you encountered at your shoppe was not Candace Anderson. It was Candra! She knew her sister was getting out soon and was reporting everything to Candace. At that moment, you and everything about your life was in danger.

Jordan couldn't tell you, because he didn't even know yet. I don't even think *he* was in as much danger as you at that time.

"The night at the beach, Jordan actually saved your life, Chris! You closed up the shoppe early. The surveillance cameras picked up Candra dropping off a small package right at the rear entrance of your shoppe. Even though she tripped the alarm, she got away. Still, she left you a 'gift'. It was a low-impact shrapnel bomb, meaning it was designed to maim or disfigure its victim. She wanted to hurt you really badly.

"The night you and Jordan had dinner when she recorded your conversation, she went to your house and waited for you, but your never went home."

This was getting to be too much to handle. If I was standing up, I would have passed out, but I slouched down in my chair and began to pant for air. I wasn't having an asthma attack, but I couldn't breathe. The air felt thick in the room for some reason, and I couldn't catch my breath. I wanted to scream, to cry, to rejoice, but I was numb and confused. Don't get me wrong, I was thankful none of her attempts came to fruition, but the thought of someone so obsessed over another person that it would drive them to do something so diabolical was insane.

"Chris, I need you to stay with me!" Tee continued filling in all the blanks until she came down to the end. Here we were at the last piece of the puzzle. We just needed to know who shot Candace. It would have been simpler if it *had* been me because I could've claimed self-defense. That would have been the end of it, but there was a missing $y$ component in this $xyz$ equation.

"Tee, I'll confess. I'll say I did it. Right now, it looks like what could be cut and dry and simple is getting complicated and muddy. I don't like muddy. I don't like complicated. These two families have been through enough, and..."

"So you think confessing to something you obviously did not do is going to make this any less 'muddy'? You think lying is going to make this go away? Are you thinking, Ms. Lackner? I want to represent you, but I will be not made a fool of at any time during this process. I thought I made this clear from the beginning! Did you not understand this?"

"Oh, I understood you loud and clear, but know this, I will lay down life for my own, and don't you ever forget that. Candace almost got her wish. She almost took me out. She was erased in the process. I am asking you to make this disappear. If you have any maternal instincts in you at all, *make this shit disappear*!" I pleaded with Tee through a constant stream of tears.

I don't know if my fists or my tears hit the table harder, but Tee wanted me to know that she was a tough person, and I was determined to show her that my mild-mannered demeanor did not mean that I was not just as tough or tougher. She was not going to win this battle. We were facing a war in the courtroom, she was being paid handsomely, and I was exhausted from it all.

I stood up from the table, nodded at Tee and told her that I would see her in court. Jenique looked at me with pleading eyes, and I sat back down just for her.

"What is it, baby?"

"Momma, I know!"

"Baby, look, we have court coming up tomorrow. Let's just get prepared for that! I suggest we all get a good night sleep so we'll be fresh in the morning."

Jordan and I retired to the guest bedroom on the first floor. We talked about everything except the case until we drifted off to sleep.

# 29

The gavel struck and the trial began. Candra pleaded guilty to attempted murder and was given a sentencing date. I was astonished as the bailiff announced we were dismissed. Nothing was even said about Candace. My mouth could have collected jackalopes it was dropped so wide open.

"Ms. Tanya Streets, please accept my most sincere apology for putting you through so much prior to this moment." In my mind, most of what we had gone through was a waste of time.

"Ms. Lackner, you didn't put me through anything. I was tired of seeing you putting yourself through so much. You needed to work through this. Whatever happened to Candace was not your concern because you did nothing to her. The focus was on you. We needed to know how you were impacted in all of this. My hope is that your prominence in the community will carry the weight this case needs and this sister will get life plus.

"Now, when it comes to you, Jordan, she's going to say that it was Candace and not her. That's fine because you don't have to worry about either of them anymore."

The three of us embraced as we exited the courtroom.

*Two Weeks Later...*

I guess fairytales really do come true. I woke up to my wedding gown hanging on the back of my bedroom door. My slippers were in place and there was a note on the night stand letting me know that the hair stylist would be arriving at 9:00 a.m.

The clock read 7:43, so there was time to shower, eat and piddle a bit before the stylist arrived. I was super excited. I wanted to call Jordan, but didn't want to jinx anything, so I just relaxed and soaked in everything. Jenique and Laticia were out and about. Marco was gathering his 'boys' and making sure he was dapper enough to give the bride away. Mom called to make sure I wasn't beside myself; I really needed to hear her voice.

"How're you feeling, Baby? You got everything you need? I know you do; I'm just asking. I don't know who's more nervous...me or you!" Even though mom was excited, she had a knack for calming my nerves.

We both snickered. I assured her that I was just fine and passing time until the big event. She told me that there was a slight change in plans but nothing to worry about. Of course I got nervous, but they had this. All I had to do was participate.

The stylists arrived twenty minutes early and immediately got to work. I had to be ready to leave by 11:00 in the outfit that would be arriving 'soon'. Needless to say, my hair was gorgeous, and I was dressed and ready to go on my mark. My chariot pulled up whisked me off to brunch with close friends who were very aware it was my special day but were unable to attend the ceremony. It was like a pre-celebration or a bridal shower. It was fun and quirky, and we all had a blast. I had cards and money pinned to me as I was loaded back into the Suburban. I got back home before 1:30 and did not have to leave until 2:45.

Talk about ready; I was standing close to the curb when the limo pulled up. I made sure all alarms were set, and I slid into the back seat of my ride. We got to the 'field of dreams' (a quaint little field off of Portsmouth Boulevard just across the Suffolk City line) to a small, waiting group of family and friends, all dressed in different shades of purple. Jordan was standing up by the Pastors, waiting for Marco to escort me to my groom. I could barely contain myself. I wanted to be like Whitney Houston and run to him, but I walked a very eye-catching, don't-you-see-me, ah-ha-I'm-glowing walk down that aisle to Jordan.

Frieda was my maid of honor, and her royal purple gown matched Marco's royal on lavender tuxedo perfectly while he stood in double duty as best man, also. Two of Jordan's brothers, Jasper and Lorenzo stood as groomsmen, and Laticia and Jenique served as bridesmaids. Duchess and Princess were flower girl and ring bearess. Jordan knew that I desired a male and a female officiant to perform the ceremony, symbolizing equality as well as unity.

I must admit, Jordan turned out to be a much stronger man than I ever imagined, especially with everything we had gone through. In the midst of all of this, he still managed to pull off this beautifully, well-orchestrated dream I painted for him in that hotel room months ago. Not only did he have a good memory, he had the resources and the desire. After all, you know what they say, 'happy wife – happy life!'

# *30*

Jordan and I decided to write our vows, and I was sure with everything we had been through, Jordan's would have been rushed or read even, but when he started speaking from the heart, I was immediately brought to tears.

"Chris, from the moment I met you, I knew you were special...unique. I learned over time that you would be the one to make my life complete. You're attractive, sassy, decisive, and smart. You're warm and caring, and you have a big heart. You love what you do, and you do what you do well. And if anyone tries to cross you, you give 'em hell. You're a trooper because you stuck by me when times were tough. You stood up for what was right, and you never gave up. I love your tenacity. I love your spirit. I love your smile and your laughter when I hear it. I love the fact that family is everything to you. I love you for allowing me to love you. I will be there for you always, no matter what life throws our way. I'll come home to you every night, and kiss you before I leave every day. I will protect you. I will guide you. I will lead you the best I can. I promise you that I will forever be a dutiful and faithful husband."

As inappropriate as it may have seemed to some, I had to give him finger snaps for that one. It was beautiful! Then I had to bring things back in and get serious.

"Jordan, I'm sorry! I don't have an eloquent poem to recite or beautiful words written out to read to you. I only have my heart, and I give it to you completely. I know we've been to hell and back, and I'm glad we made it back to each other because I can't think of anyone else I would rather spend forever with. You have shown me a love that will not wither even through adversity, and that speaks volumes. You have shown me strength and courage like no other, and that means the world to me. I thank you, and I love you. Not only have you accepted me in your heart, but you've enveloped my children, and you've shared two beautiful daughters with me, as well. I love you for all that you are. I love you for all that you stand for. I love you for all that you believe in. I love you for loving me. I have faith and confidence that you will be the husband that God requires you to be for me is every aspect, and I will be loyal, faithful, understanding, loving, dutiful, respectful, and as submissive as I can be for all eternity to you. I love you. Now, for the last time, in front of God and everybody, I'm sorry! You know I don't give too many of those out."

I had to end all of the tearful moments with a little chuckle. But, it was good to see Jordie smile a relaxed smile for a change.

After we exchanged vows, the Officiants directed us in exchanging rings. Then we were pronounced husband and wife by both of the Officiants just before 3:30. The sunset was scheduled for 4:43. Jordan wanted enough daylight for everyone to mingle for a bit, get gorgeous evening wedding photos, and then see their way back to their cars as we snuck off for our honeymoon. It worked!

We could have chosen anywhere in the world to go for our honeymoon, Ecuador, Cancun, Argentina, Paris, anywhere! I wanted to go to Washington, D. C., somewhere where there were lots of people and we could get lost in the crowds, yet be close enough to not lose sight of each other. I didn't want to escape crazy; I wanted to replace our crazy with a different kind of crazy.

We stayed at The Jefferson on the eighth floor and enjoyed the view overlooking the city. When we arrived in the wee hours of the morning, the city lights made everything look so vibrant and lively. I was caught up in amazement of the beauty of where we were, who I was with, and the fact that I was finally Mrs. Jordan Hines or Mrs. Mario Antoine Naples. I didn't know if he wanted to go back to his birth-given name or remain Jordan. That was something we could talk about in the future. Right now, I was relishing the fact that I was this loving man's wife. This man that had fought for me, got cut for me, and hid evidence for me, was now my better half. *No man (or woman)* was *ever* gonna come between that.

I gazed out of the window, thinking how amazing my life has been, even in the unpleasant moments. There were the valleys in the rollercoaster ride, but coming up out of them was what made it all worth it. Sometimes, it's not that you accomplished your goal; it's that you were able to overcome all the obstacles that were in the way trying to keep you from getting to that final prize.

Jordan came up behind me and lightly kissed the nape of my neck. His fingertips traced my shoulders and followed the curves of my arms down past my wrists to my fingertips where we locked digits. His body pressed firmly against mine, and all I could do was close my eyes and give into the gentle breaths escaping his lips before his tongue softly traced the outline of my left ear. I pulled away for a moment because he was nearing one of the places I had been shot.

"Baby, relax. Your scars are my scars. Let me take care of you. Let me heal you. I promised you that I would never hurt you again - I won't!"

"It's not only that, Baby. I just realized that we haven't been intimate in months. I remember you told me at the hospital that would give me as much time as I needed, and you haven't even attempted to get close to me in this way since. I'm not complaining; I think this is my way of thanking you for being so understanding!"

"You had to get through this ordeal without any distractions, *and* I wanted to be as pure and I could possibly be for you on this night. It was hard sometimes to maintain my composure with you so sexy and all. If you feel anything like I do, and I'm sure you do, you're ready to...for lack of better words right now...tear up some shit!" Jordan growled playfully.

All I could do was laugh and fall into his arms. He was right; I was ready to move some furniture and do serious damage. Things were definitely hot for the first two days. Then came the heavy as we started future life discussions.

"Jordie, I don't know if you're even aware or not, but according to your paperwork, I may be married to two men. You have legal documentation under both names, so....."

"We've been married, what, three days, and you're cheating on me already? Damn!" Even though Jordie was playful in his retort, there was an awkward truth in the statement.

"Cute, but seriously, you know what kind of person I am. Who am I supposed to be? Or am I expected to live in duality as well?"

"Well, you are my wife, and you have as much say so in this matter as I do, so how would you like to be known? Because you can call me anything. I just want you to be happy and comfortable, Chris."

"I met you as Jordan, but I honestly started rehearsing Mario or Antoine or Toine over the past two weeks. I think because I know that Jordan was the name of your dog, I wanted to try your true name, but when I look at you, I think about getting lost in you, like swimming in the Jordan River and just letting go of all of my inhibitions. I'm able to do that with you. It's not that Mario doesn't have meaning, but Jordan has so much more meaning - to me! It's a lifeline!"

"Okay. How about I'm Jordan, and since my man, here, seems to like it in dark places so much – kind of like my past – we'll call him Mario.

"That works! In that case, I think Mario and I need to have a proper introduction, face to face. Don't you agree?" I offered myself to my husband on my knees.

Jordan's River

# MEET YOUR AUTHOR

Catherine, affectionately known as Kittee was raised in Wilson, North Carolina and now lives in Portsmouth, Virginia. She is a single-parent of three children and two grandchildren and very involved in their lives.

She has had a passion for writing since she was seven years young, with some personal encouragement from Maya Angelou. She's experimented with many forms of poetry, on to short stories to now her first novel. Of all the genres she seems to have found her voice in storytelling; Not only does she write from experience, but she writes with pride and passion...she pours love onto each and every page hoping to capture the essence of the stories and the interest of the reader.

Other published works by this writer include:
Erotic Adventures in Kitteeville,
Erotic Adventures by Candlelight,
2014 Random Thoughts of Sexee Kittee
2015 Random Thoughts of Sexee Kittee

Jordan's River

colophon
Brought to you by Wider Perspectives Publishing, care of James
Wilson, with the mission of advancing the poetry and creative
community of Hampton Roads, Virginia.
See our production of works from ...

Tanya Cunningham-Jones
        (Scientific Eve)
Terra Leigh
Ray Simmons
S.A. Borders-Shoemaker
Taz Waysweete'
Bobby K. (The Poor Man's Poet)
J. Scott Wilson (TEECH!)
Charles Wilson
Gloria Darlene Mann
Neil Spirtas
Zach Crowe
Jorge Mendez & JT Williams
Sarah Eileen Williams
Stephanie Diana (Noftz)
the Hampton Roads
        Artistic Collective
Jason Brown (Drk Mtr)
Martina Champion
Tony Broadway
Ken Sutton
Crickyt J. Expression
Lisa M. Kendrick
Cassandra IsFree
Nich (Nicholis Williams)
Samantha Geovjian Clarke
Natalie Morison-Uzzle
Shanya Lady S

... and others to come soon.

We promote and support the artists
of the 757
*from the seats, from the stands,*
*from the snapping fingers and*
*clapping hands*
*from the pages, and the stages*
 *and now we pass them forth*
*to the ages*

Check for the above artists on
FaceBook, the Virginia Poetry
Online channel on YouTube, and
other social media.

Hampton Roads Artistic Collective is the
non-profit extension of WPP and strives
to simultaneously support worthy causes
in Hampton Roads and the creative
artists.

www.ingramcontent.com/pod-product-compliance
Lightning Source LLC
Chambersburg PA
CBHW020658260626
47157CB00008B/3074